THE MILLENNIUM

THE MILLENNIUM

A COMEDY
OF THE YEAR 2000

BY
UPTON SINCLAIR

Quality Paperback Book Club
New York

FOREWORD

THIS little farce comedy of the future was originally a four-act drama. It was written seventeen years ago, immediately after the Helicon Hall fire, as a means of diverting the writer's mind from thoughts of that tragic event. The play was accepted for production by David Belasco, but years of delay took place, and finally the manuscript was submitted to other managers, and in the course of time all copies were lost. If this should come to the eye of anyone having a copy, the writer will be glad to hear from him.

The present version had been sketched out for an editor friend who wanted to publish the story as a serial. Readers of an observant turn of mind will detect the outlines of the play. Act I was laid in the Roof Garden of the Pleasure Palace; Act II in the Entrance Hall at the foot of the ninety-nine flights of stairs; Act III in the kitchen of the Consolidated Hotel; Act IV at the Country Estate of the Lumley-Gothams. New material, not in the play, was supplied between the last two acts. It is amusing to note that many details about airplanes and wireless telephones, imaginary when the play was written, are now everyday affairs to us all!

For the original suggestion of this story the author is indebted to Mr. Fred D. Warren, from whom he purchased the idea.

PASADENA, CALIFORNIA.
   February, 1924.

THE MILLENNIUM

IT was shortly before the hour set for the opening ceremonies, when Billy Kingdon stepped out of the elevator upon the roof-garden of the palace, and stood for a moment gazing about him, awe-stricken.

He had read long accounts of the structure which the ruling-class had reared for its pleasure in the midst of Central Park. He had read of the elaborate ceremonies with which the opening was to be celebrated. He stared now at the towering columns, eight or ten feet thick; and at the fairy-like fresco of lights in the glass roof, so high overhead that it seemed to outreach the stars. He realized that the gold tessellated floor beneath his feet was a hundred stories in the air—nearly half a mile above the teeming city of New York.

The head butler, gorgeous in the uniform of the upper-servant caste, stepped up to demand his business.

"Captain of the aeroplane," answered Billy.

"Your pass?"

He took it from his pocket, and the head butler inspected it. At the same moment the major-domo of the Pleasure Palace stepped up.

"You understand," he said, "that Mr. Lumley-Gotham is in the building? Your pass has to be counter-signed."

"I have had that attended to," was Billy's reply.

The other took the paper and scrutinized it carefully, comparing its number and signatures with certain entries in his notebook. It had been only a week ago that some anarchists had made an attempt upon the life of Lumley-Gotham, and police precautions had been redoubled.

As the major-domo handed back the pass, he looked more cordially at this handsome young fellow, wearing the simple grey uniform of the engineering caste. "You are young for a master-aeronaut."

"I have worked hard," Billy answered.

"You have the most important assignment of your career to-night. Good luck to you."

"Where is the aeroplane?" Billy inquired, and the head butler pointed to one side of the roof-garden, where through the open spaces between the snow-white columns, the light framework of the machine could be dimly made out. Billy hastened towards it, and at the edge of the landing-stage stopped and gazed at it.

He loved this marvellous aeroplane, in the designing of which he had assisted. She was five hundred feet long, and balanced herself; no storm could affect her; she turned somersaults in the air without danger to her passengers. For over a hundred years the world's cleverest minds had been devoted to making the perfect flying-machine, and now, in the year 2000, there she stood—" The Monarch of the Air! " A thousand miles an hour was her speed, and at dawn she was to take a part of the chosen ones of the earth, the guests of Mrs. Lumley-Gotham, following the sunrise in a journey around the world.

Billy turned his gaze for a few moments to the panorama of the city, upon which he looked as if from a mountain-height. Then he gazed into the ball-room, whose walls were a blend of tropical flowers and soft, golden lights. There were lackeys, in gold and azure uniforms and powdered wigs, moving about, swinging censers. The sound of faint music was heard, played by an orchestra far off in the city, conveyed by electricity to every portion of the hundred-story palace. Following the movement and rhythm of the music, the lights in the roof varied continuously in intensity and colour—for the artists of this time had worked out the problem of harmonizing music and light.

Billy's wondering thoughts were suddenly interrupted. There was a rustle of skirts behind him, and a voice, low and agitated— " Billy Kingdon! "

He turned, and gave a suppressed cry: " Helen! "

The girl shrank back into the shadow of one of the pillars. " Billy! What does this mean? " she cried.

" It means," said he, with a laugh, " that I am the captain of the aeroplane! "

" Billy Kingdon! "

" My name is Smith, now; Henry Smith."

" But you will be recognized! It was madness for you to come! "

" I have changed a lot in five years, Helen. There is no need for you to worry."

" But my father is to be here to-night! "

" Yes," said Billy, with a smile, " the

major-domo did not fail to inform me of that."

" But don't you know that he would have you killed, if he discovered you? He would think it was another plot against his life. Oh, why should you take such a risk? "

" I have taken many risks," answered the other. " I risked my life when I deserted my own class to join the labour caste. I risked it again when I became an engineer without revealing my true identity. I have grown used to such risks."

" But why do an insane thing like this? Don't you know that even my husband might come here to-night? "

" Don't talk to me about him! " exclaimed the youth.

" But think what he would do if he recognized you! Why be so reckless? "

The young man waved his hand towards the aeroplane. " There is the reason. The Monarch of the Air! "

" You care that much about an aeroplane? "

" Look at the curve of her wings! Wait until you have felt the quiver of her as she moves! " He laughed excitedly. But then his manner changed. He leaned forward,

studying the woman's face.   " Do you believe
what I am saying? "

" Why not? "

He took a step towards her.   " No, Helen!
I came for something else! "   And as she
shrank away: " I came for you! " he
whispered.   " Answer me.   You still love
me? "

" I dare not answer, Billy—you know it."

" Because you are married? "

" Partly that——"

" Helen, that was no marriage, it was a sale!
You know he did not love you; you knew it
then.   You knew that he wanted the daughter
of Lumley-Gotham, he wanted to be your
father's master."

" Don't bring all that up!" she cried.   " I
can't bear it! "

" I bring all that up," he said, " because
I want you to come with me."

" But where?   Where could we go that my
husband would not find us?   Billy, he would
never give us up.   He would hunt us out, and
when he had found us he would torture us to
death!   You don't realize how he has things
organized—all the machinery of spying! "

Billy laughed.   " No one knows better than

I," he said. "I help to keep his world going."

"But do you realize his persistence? It is madness to think that I could escape! He would know it was you who came for me."

"Listen," said Billy, quickly. "I have not come without a plan. I am captain of the aeroplane. I will be the master of their fate and of our own for twenty-four hours. I will be the only man on board who knows how to run the aeroplane. I will pretend that the machinery is out of order. When we are over Central Africa, I will alight in a lonely place, and step out to examine the propeller. You will follow me, without being seen by anyone. I will set the machinery so that it will start—they will rise in the air again, without me. In the excitement, you will not be missed. They will think you have fallen overboard."

The girl stood in anxious thought. "But, Billy," she said, "what will become of them?"

"The aeroplane is self-balancing. She is as safe in the air as a cork on the surface of the water. They will drift until they are found. They will communicate with the nearest rescue station by their wireless telephone. They will be located at once—we have new machinery for such work. The rescue party will reach them in a few minutes, and will put a pilot on board to take them home. Can you imagine that the world would let anything happen to Lumley-Gotham, its owner?"

Helen was silent. The plan was a mad one, yet it might succeed. "What would become of us," she whispered, "alone in the wilderness?"

"We shall have food and weapons. I have provided everything that is necessary. Your husband has not yet perfected a device for locating a solitary man and woman in the heart of Central Africa!"

Seeing that she was wavering, he started towards her, pleading, "Helen, what else is there in life for us? I have travelled to the ends of the earth, trying to forget you. I have risked my life a hundred times—but apparently I cannot die, and I know that I cannot live without you."

He saw the terror in her countenance. "Oh, wait, wait!" she exclaimed. "Give me time; you must let me think it over." She caught herself together and drew back, for it was an unheard of thing for a woman of her class to be talking with a low caste man.

He answered. "You have several hours to think it over. But let me tell you this: Whatever you decide, the aeroplane will stop, and I shall be left behind. The only question is, whether you step out upon the ground with me, or whether you go off with the rest. You understand that?"

"Yes, yes," she whispered. And then looking about and seeing a servant approaching, she turned and moved swiftly away.

The time for the great ceremonial was drawing near. One or two at a time the guests emerged from the elevators, and wandered about, gazing at the decorations, or seating themselves upon the uncomfortable gold settees. Among the first to come was de Puyster, wearing the uniform of the newspaper reporters' guild, a plum-coloured dress suit with long coat-tails and large gold buttons. His tie was of rose-point lace, and he wore high-heeled shoes and coloured gloves; he spoke with many affectations and grimaces, combined with the business-like air of a man of affairs.

He presented his card to Tuttle, the head butler, who in a clear voice announced his name: "Mr. Harold de Puyster, society reporter of the Universal Press Association."

"Pass properly counter-signed?" inquired the major-domo.

"Yes, sir," said the other. And de Puyster, after many formal bows to the guests about him, proceeded to a telephone at one side. Billy could distinctly hear every word —there being a sounding-board provided, so that the arriving guests might know in advance what the newspapers of the world were saying about them.

"Hello!" began de Puyster. "Universal Press Association. Hello!—city department?" He spoke rapidly, for the wireless telephone service was automatic and instantaneous. "This is de Puyster. You have the proofs for the ten o'clock extras? Read them, please." He paused to listen. "No, no. That's a mistake. That's for the regular ten o'clock edition. The copy for the extra begins, ' The supreme moment in the history of the social year has struck to-night, upon the occasion of the opening festivities in the new Pleasure Palace.' You have it? Ah, yes!

Now find the seventh paragraph. 'Never before in the history of Metropolitan society has so exclusive and august an assemblage met under circumstances so appropriate and striking.' Yes, that is it. After that paragraph insert my comments upon the events of the evening. All ready! " And he laughed. " Ah, yes! Trust me to make them spicy! "

Two guests emerged from the elevator. One wore a costume even more eccentric than de Puyster's—the uniform of the poet's guild. He had scores of jewelled rings upon his fingers, and carried a ribbon-tied manuscript in his hand. The young woman by his side was fat and languid, and wore a gown cut low, with heels upon her shoes so high that it seemed she was walking upon stilts.

The head butler announced : " Miss Eloise Lumley-Gotham. Mr. Reginald Simpkins."

The voice of de Puyster began at the telephone : " Among the guests who arrived early was the beautiful and charming younger daughter of the hostess. Miss Eloise Lumley-Gotham was clad in a resplendent cloth-of-silver gown, studded with diamonds. She wore her famous jewels, with the tiara left her by her great-aunt, the Duchesse de Petit-

B

bourse. She was accompanied by Mr. Reginald Simpkins, Poet Laureate of Society, whose noble ' Ode to Private Property ' was the sensation of last season. It is whispered that the author has not been content to rest upon his laurels, but will grace the festivities of the night with a sonnet entitled, ' The Line of Lumley-Gotham.' "

Eloise had stood listening to what de Puyster had to say. " Well, Reggie," she asked, " what do you think of our ball-room? "

Reggie, being a poet, was permitted to admire. " Gorgeous—gorgeous ! A structure which has cost a hundred and thirty seven millions ! And what an inspiration in the name ! The Pleasure Palace ! "

They moved on, and the voice of the head butler was heard again. " Miss Sarita Knickerbocker-Smythe."

The lady who entered was stout and of uncertain age, wearing many jewels, and bowing with stateliness to the guests. De Puyster proclaimed : " Miss Sarita, the heiress of the Knickerbocker-Smythes, graced the occasion with her usual resplendence."

Miss Sarita started. " Oh dear me ! They have sent that odious de Puyster again ! "

" His Grace, the Lord Bishop of Harlem," proclaimed Tuttle.

The Lord Bishop was corpulent and wore a pleasant smile, walking with his hands over his paunch. His robes were scarlet and purple, with brocade and jewels and a long train.

" Good evening, my friends," he said, and as de Puyster said nothing, he sidled up to him and coughed softly. " Ah, good evening, de Puyster. You—er—I believe you overlooked me."

" Ah, surely, Your Grace! " said the other, politely. Then to the telephone: " His Grace, the Lord Bishop of Harlem, next graced the occasion with his presence."

The Lord Bishop turned to Eloise. " My dear young lady, what a great happiness it must be to your mother to be able to provide her friends with such a sumptuous entertainment! How proud she ought to be."

" Oh," answered Eloise, " she's proud enough, no doubt."

" Um—ah—yes! " stammered the Lord Bishop. " Truly, ha, ha! " And then to Reggie: " How clever our young people are getting to be! " As Reggie paid no attention to him, he began addressing Eloise again, with renewed unction. "But truly, you know, one cannot cease to marvel at the wonders of modern mechanical skill. Think of it—two thousand feet in the air! Do you consider it safe?"

Reggie did not wish to be outdone. "How long society has pined for this very thing— some place that was absolutely apart, where the chosen few might gather, secure from all intrusion! A place where the feet of the vulgar have never trod—where not even the thought of the mob could penetrate!"

"Mr. Lumley-Gotham, junior," proclaimed Tuttle.

The guests turned and watched the approach of a thin and dyspeptic-looking youth, who condescended to greet no one save his sister. De Puyster's voice, with special solemnity, pronounced: "Next came that fortunate young man to whom will some day fall the ownership of more than half the vested wealth of the United States. He wore the diamond star recently presented by the students of his Sunday school class."

"Mother is late, is she not?" remarked Eloise.

The young man replied, " Mother is *never* late."

" But I mean—the time," said the girl.

" Mother *makes* the time," was the answer of the fortunate young man, as he strolled towards the ball-room.

" Mrs. St. Erskine Granville," proclaimed the head butler ; and there entered the girl with whom Billy had talked—she had gone below in order to escape attention, and now made her formal entrance. Slender, with steady brown eyes, she was less eccentrically dressed than the others. To Billy, who stood gazing from the shadows of his aeroplane, she was the most beautiful object that ever graced a ball-room.

But de Puyster apparently did not agree, for there was a touch of malice in his voice as he proclaimed : " The elder daughter of the line of Lumley-Gotham next appeared, the charming wife of St. Erskine Granville, Secretary of State and Councillor-in-Chief of Mr. Lumley-Gotham. Her costume was suited to her peculiar style of beauty."

Eloise had been staring at her sister, making no attempt to conceal the displeasure upon her countenance. " Helen ! " she exclaimed.

" Surely here at least you might have worn some appropriate costume ! "

" My dear," said the other quietly, " if you know how much effort it cost me to come at all, you'd be glad to see me in any costume."

" I declare," said Eloise, " I can't understand you ! "

" That is no new complaint of yours," replied the other, as she moved towards the ball-room.

Meantime the Bishop had sidled over towards de Puyster and nodded to him. " Don't forget about the wine ! "

Whereupon the telephone took the message : " It is rumoured that the great authority, His Grace, the Lord Bishop of Harlem, has been in consultation with the official bootleggers. In particular, the wines of the third banquet are entirely of his selection. If this be true, Mrs. Lumley-Gotham may rest assured that this part of her entertainment will be long remembered by her guests."

There was a general murmur from the guests. " Ah, Bishop, that is really interesting ! " cried Reggie.

And Eloise broke in : " While you've been

advising about wines, I hope you've not forgotten to give mother your recipe for deviled skylarks' livers."

The Bishop winked slyly, and his voice fell to a whisper. "I have promised to say nothing about the menu—but you shall have your livers."

The voice of the head butler was heard once more: "Mr. St. Erskine Granville."

Silence fell as there entered a man of aristocratic aspect, with a smooth-shaven ascetic face. If for a moment this face had a genial expression, you felt that he was merely playing with some victim—and that contempt was near to its surface.

He was regarded by the others with fear only slightly veiled.

The poet came sidling up to him. "Good evening, Mr. Granville." At the same time the voice of de Puyster rang out: "Mr. St. Erskine Granville, for the first time in several months shaking off the cares of state, favoured this resplendent function with his presence——"

Granville spoke—addressing Reggie, and nodding towards de Puyster. "Tell him to stop that."

"I beg pardon?" said Reggie, not understanding.

"Tell him to leave me out." And the poet hurried over to de Puyster, who hastened to cancel this portion of his gossip.

His Grace, the Lord Bishop of Harlem, now came up to pay his respects. "Good evening, Bishop," said Granville, and added, with a smile, "You are several stories nearer heaven to-night."

"Our Secretary of State is in a merry mood!" laughed the Bishop. "But you should have waited until you had me in the aeroplane."

"I shall have new jests then for our sky-pilot!"

"Ha, ha! Well done!"

Then came Sarita, stout and ugly. "Have you anything to say to me?" she inquired, coquettishly.

"Be assured, my dear lady, that if I were capable of the grand passion, the object of it could be none other than yourself."

Eloise and her poet laughed in chorus. The latter's laughter continued for a moment longer, and Granville's glance rested upon him. "Reggie, does it never occur to you to wonder whether you are happy—or only think you are happy?"

The Secretary of State then turned to Eloise, who inquired, "Did you know that Helen is here?"

"What! My virgin wife?"

"Yes."

"What can that mean? Have all the social problems been solved—all the proletariat educated?" He looked about and seeing his wife, went towards her. "Well, Mrs. Granville! to what do we owe this chaste pleasure?"

"In part to the fact that I had no idea that *you* would be here."

The Lord Bishop stepped in. "Helen," he pleaded, "may I speak to you?"

"What is it?"

"I ask a favour of you. Since this fortunate meeting has occurred, I ask you to reflect how it would please your honoured mother if you and your husband would consent to appear together in the grand march. Think——"

"Why should you concern yourself with this?"

"Is that not my office? To preserve the home—the sacred institution of marriage——"

" Marriage," exclaimed Helen, "involves a give and take. Ask him what he has ever given to me."

She waited, while the Lord Bishop turned to her husband.

" Ask her," continued the Secretary of State, " what she has ever given to me."

" I gave him the control of my father's fortune—the mastery of the state! The ability to dominate millions of other lives, to break their will to his! To watch them writhing—to crush them into impotence, and then mock them because they are impotent. That is what he sought in marriage, and he obtained it. Now let him enjoy it!"

With these words she turned with a gesture of scorn—while her husband laughed aloud. " A lady with a rapier tongue, Bishop."

" Yet a lady with a mind!" protested the other. " A mind——"

" She seeks to read the riddles of God!" said Granville. " And they have no answers —they are jests."

The guests moved on to inspect the upper ball-room, and for a while the roof-garden was empty, save for the lackeys, and the head butler at his station. Some minutes passed, when Helen Granville re-entered, and after looking about to make sure that no one was observing her, moved towards the landing-stage. Concealed in the shadows of the aeroplane, she whispered softly, "Billy!"

In an instant, as it seemed, Billy Kingdon was gazing up at her. "Well?"

"I have thought it over," she said. "I want to beg you to give it up."

"Never!" he exclaimed.

"But you must! I say you must! He will find us; he will kill us surely."

"I have told you what I mean to do, Helen. The question for you is: Will you join me?"

"I have made up my mind," she answered. "I will not join you. I will not even go on the ride."

His answer was to spring up and catch her by the hand. "Helen! I love you!"

She resisted, but he held her fast. He held her more with the look in his eyes than with the strength of his clasp; and at last she surrendered—her struggle ceased, and he took her in his arms. "Billy," she whispered. "this is death!"

" It is all that life holds for me! " he answered.

" Billy, listen to me. I ask you once more—for the last time—go away! Go now! "

" And for the last time, I say no."

" If you love me——"

" I love you too much! "

" Billy, listen——" she began, and her sentence was not finished. St. Erskine Granville stepped out suddenly from behind a pillar and confronted the two. " So this is our runaway, Billy Kingdon! And in a labourer's uniform! "

Helen started in horror; then, catching herself together, she took a step towards her husband. " Listen——" she began.

" I have already listened! " he replied. Then, with his mocking smile, " My virgin wife! "

He turned to Billy. " How do you come here? " he demanded sharply.

" I am captain of the aeroplane," said the other without emotion.

" I see," said Granville. " Under what name? "

" Not my own."

"Then you have taken your life into your hands?"

"So I understand," was the reply. "It is not the first time—as you know."

Granville stood looking at his victim with curiosity. "What does all this mean?" he asked.

Billy's reply came with a slight smile of contempt. "I could not explain it to you," he said. "You had best call it madness, and let it go at that."

Said Granville: "I was young once. I knew the madness of young love."

"They took Helen from me and gave her to you," said Billy. "But there were other reasons for my running away. There is in this world of yours nothing a man could devote his energies to. Look at this scene to-night—these strutting puppets, these gilded dolls!"

"Someone must rule them," answered the other, with his quiet smile.

"Perhaps," said the young man. "That was your nature. It was not mine. I went away."

"To what?"

Billy waved his hand towards the aeroplane.

" There, at least, is something real.   To understand her, to be her master—that seemed to me a man's job ! "

" To run a machine ! " sneered Granville. " A child's toy !   And you, who were born to power, who might have walked the quarter-deck of the Ship of State ! "

" You made it into a slave-ship ! " was the answer.   " It interests you.   It doesn't interest me.   I wondered how it was with Helen ; and I came to-night to find out."

" You found out, it would seem," said Granville.

" I did," was the reply.   " I found that she agrees with me.   And to-night we shall leave."

" What ? " cried the other.   He started to raise his hand to summon his guards.   But Billy, who had been watching him, drew a weapon.   " If you move a finger, you die ! "

Helen sprang forward with a cry.   " Billy ! No ! "

There was a silence.   At last Billy spoke, his voice low.   " Helen," he said, " it is his life or mine."

" No ! " she cried.

He went on : " You have to choose between

us. He has murdered millions of people—he, the crusher of revolutions. I can kill him now, without a sound, and we can escape in the aeroplane. But if he lives, he will take my life."

" He shall not! " she exclaimed.

"He will do it," insisted Billy. " Let there be no question about that."

" I will appeal to my father! He will save you! "

" I will be dead before your father ever hears of me."

Helen turned to her husband, whose face, in spite of his peril, still wore its easy smile. " Granville——" she began.

But Billy stopped her. " Don't waste your time like that! Which of us is to live? Choose! "

She cried in horror: " How could I be happy if I had my husband's blood upon my hands? "

Billy stood, still watching Granville. Gradually his face set in a stern look. " Is that your last word? "

There was a silence. " Is that your last? "

Helen spoke in a faint whisper. " You must not kill him."

Whereupon Billy, without a sound, put his weapon into his pocket, and turning his back, moved towards the aeroplane. Granville raised his hand, and his guards, who were never out of sight, leaped forward and flung themselves upon the youth. To the cries of his wife the Secretary of State paid no attention whatever, and to his guards he said merely : " Solitary confinement." While Helen hurried away to seek her father, he stood smiling to himself.

From scores of elevators the guests were now emerging upon the roof-garden, arrayed in costumes of brilliant colour and extravagant design, glittering with jewels of every hue. Their senses were overwhelmed by peals of thunderous music, which seemed to flood the sky ; this music came to a climax, and broke into a stately march, whereupon the guests turned towards the elevators. There came out four men in gorgeous livery, keeping step to the music, and bearing a splendid palanquin, in which sat an old lady, fat, painted, and gorgeous with jewels. Her costume was of crimson velvet, about two-thirds of it covered with diamonds. Her corsage was a veritable

armour-plate of diamonds, and there was a
diamond crown, and diamond bracelets half-
way up her arms. In solemn tones came the
voice of the head butler: " Mrs. Lumley-
Gotham ! "

The assembly bowed reverently as the great
lady was borne to the centre of the room.
The attendants set down the palanquin,
and stood saluting, while in one voice
spoke the guests: " Hail, Mrs. Lumley-
Gotham ! "

The old lady rose feebly upon the arms of
two of the attendants. Her voice was shrill
and cracked, but it penetrated the enormous
room because of a megaphone device which
she had concealed in her corsage. " Welcome,
friends, to the Pleasure Palace ! "

Then came the voice of de Puyster at the
telephone: " The glorious strains of the
Citizens' Alliance march now hailed the
approach of the hostess of the occasion—Mrs.
Viviana Athelstan de Smithkins Lumley-
Gotham, to whose munificence society owes
the existence of this temple of hospitality, a
temple preserved for ever from all contact
with vulgar life, and dedicated to the service
of those to whom God in His infinite wisdom

has entrusted the care of the property interests of the country ! "

The ceremony completed, the great lady sank into her seat again, and the Lord Bishop advanced to pay his respects. " Ah, Mrs. Lumley-Gotham, how charming you appear! It fills me with the emotions of youth to see you! I would that all your jealous rivals might be present."

Then came the poet laureate. " Condescend, oh gracious Mistress of Society, to receive this tribute, which is destined to perpetuate the memory of your munificence, and make known to future generations the majesty of the line of Lumley-Gotham ! "

" Thank you, Reggie," said Mrs. Lumley-Gotham's cracked voice. She took the manuscript from his hand.

" I shall hope," continued the poet, " to have occasion to recite it to your company. By the way, Eloise and I have completed the minuet you designed for us. Will you see us in the last steps? "

He began to execute some fancy dance-steps; but in the course of the procedure he turned his back, and Mrs. Lumley-Gotham signalled the bearers, who picked up the palanquin and proceeded to the ball-room, leaving him dancing, and the other guests laughing at his discomfiture.

Amid the buzz of excited chatter there came suddenly the sharp peal of a trumpet, deafening to the ear. Silence fell while the guests stood staring at each other.

"Oh dear me, what a nuisance!" exclaimed Eloise.

"Wouldn't you think he'd have the decency to leave us alone to-night?" cried Sarita.

"My dear young lady!" protested the Lord Bishop. "Isn't he to see the Pleasure Palace he has paid for?"

"Let him see it without driving his guests about like sheep!" was Sarita's response.

With the exception of Granville, the company hurried away into the ball-room, leaving the great entrance-hall empty. A death-like silence fell; while from the elevators emerged three trumpeters, in comparatively simple uniforms. They went, one to each of the entrances of the great hall, and blew another warning blast. From a second elevator emerged six men, carrying tiny weapons which represented the highest achievement of the military art in the year 2000; weapons which could be carried in a man's vest-pocket, and which would, by means of radium emanations, bring instant death to any person at whom they were aimed.

The guards separated, peering here and there, above, below; examining every corner of the room, and finally stationing themselves at the entrances. Then again fell silence, until another elevator came, out of which there emerged an old man, bald and toothless, with a sharp, wizened face. It was Lumley-Gotham himself—the present owner of more than half the United States of the Western Hemisphere, and nominal master of civilization. He was the great-great-great-grandson of the Oil King, and looked like his famous progenitor.

Lumley-Gotham's character had two attributes—avarice and fear. The former showed itself frequently, the latter showed always. He gazed here and there as he moved, and never for long without looking behind him nervously. Assisted by two attendants, he tottered to a gold settee in the middle of the room, and sank into it with a weary sigh.

St. Erskine Granville, his Secretary of State, came forward with a friendly smile. "Good evening." After a pause, he added, "A beautiful sight."

"Yes," said Lumley-Gotham, wearily, "I suppose so." But he did not look at it.

"Will you see Jessup now?" the other inquired.

"I am tired," said the old man. "I want to rest."

"But this is a matter of importance, if you remember."

"All right," replied Lumley-Gotham, knowing it was useless to protest. "Send for him."

Granville turned to one of the guards. "Summon the Director of the Department of Inventions."

A moment later a second guard approached and whispered to him, after which he said to Lumley-Gotham, "Your son wishes to see you, sir."

"Has he been searched?" inquired Lumley-Gotham.

"He has been searched," said the other.

"Very well," was the reply.

Another guard approached, and made a

signal. "Your seventh meal is ready," said Granville.

"All right," responded the old man, feebly.

Lumley-Gotham, junior, stood before his father and bowed low. "How do you do, father?" he said, respectfully.

"Very badly," snapped the other. "What do you want?"

"Why—I merely wished to see you," stammered the youth.

"Rot!" said the old man.

"I don't wish you to forget me entirely, you know."

"No, I suppose not."

"Father!" the young man exclaimed. "You don't look well! Let me suggest—don't take that ride in the aeroplane to-night. You might get air-sick again."

The Secretary of State interposed. "The ride has been ordered by your father's physician."

"I need diversion," quavered the father. "Aren't you going along?"

"What?" cried the son. "I ride in an aeroplane?"

"There is no danger," said the other.

"Every ship has been cleared from the sky —the whole air will be ours."

"Even the night-mails will be stopped," Granville added. "There can be no collision."

"Father," pleaded the young man, "I beg you not to go!"

"But why not?" cried Lumley-Gotham himself, and looked helplessly at his Secretary of State, as if asking the latter to defend him.

"Sir," said Granville, "are you not aware of the physician's order that your father is not to be disturbed at meal-times?"

One of the guards had approached, bearing a small golden tray. Upon this was a golden dish containing a dozen tablets. Granville took the tray, and stepping between Lumley-Gotham and his son, said to the former, "Help yourself."

"How many do I have?" the old man asked.

"One."

He stretched out a trembling, skinny hand, moving uncertainly from one to another of the tablets. He selected two, and offered them to one of the guards. "You eat these," he said.

The man took them obediently and
swallowed them, the old man watching
narrowly to be sure that he did not slip them
up his sleeve. There was a pause while he
watched for results.

Finally he took up another, eyed it hesi-
tatingly, and then held it out to his son.
" You eat that," he commanded.

Lumley-Gotham, junior, complied meekly;
after which his father took up another tablet,
and held it in his hand, signalling to Granville
to remove the tray. " I will eat mine in a
few minutes," he said.

The lackey bore off the food, and another
approached and whispered to Granville, who
announced, " Jessup, the Director of the
Department of Inventions."

" Has he been searched? " inquired Lumley-
Gotham.

" He has been searched."

At this moment the guard who was carrying the tray accidentally let it fall. Lumley-
Gotham started in terror. " Oh, my God! "
he exclaimed. " What does it mean? Has
that man been poisoned. Bring him back
here and let me see."

" It is not the same man who ate the food,"

said the Secretary of State. But the other was not satisfied until the servant had returned and been looked over.

Jessup entered : a stout and imposing personage in a resplendent uniform, covered with jewelled orders. He bowed ceremoniously to the master of the world, saying "At your service, sir."

"I want to talk to you," said Lumley-Gotham, sharply.

"Yes, sir."

"It has to do," broke in Granville, "with the new investigations which your department is conducting into the sources of radium. Mr. Lumley-Gotham is very nervous about them."

"For what reason, sir?"

"They are dangerous," said Granville, taking from his pocket a newspaper clipping. "This article states that Professor Holcombe has discovered a new element, which he calls radiumite, and this develops a power of an intensity never known before, penetrating all substances, and destructive to all animal life. Is that true?"

"It is, sir," answered the man.

"Well," exclaimed Granville, "I should

think that you would perceive the meaning of such a thing to Mr. Lumley-Gotham."

" In what way, sir? "

" Why, suppose this radiumite were to fall into the hands of some anarchist or madman. What protection could there be against assassination? "

Lumley-Gotham shuddered. Jessup started to explain, but the Secretary of State commanded sternly, " Let this dangerous work cease."

" But, sir," pleaded the other, "think what this radiumite means! Here is power enough to turn all the wheels of industry in the country! And think of what wealth it will create! Why, sir, from a single thimbleful of sea-water, Professor Holcombe can extract sufficient power to drive a freight airship around the world. Think of it! And it is all yours! "

Lumley-Gotham's eyes had suddenly begun to shine with excitement. " Why did you not tell me that? " he cried.

" My report has been in Mr. Granville's hands for a week," answered Jessup.

" I will tell you what you must do," said the old man. " We can't stop the work, but

Professor Holcombe must devise me some method of protection against this radiumite. And meantime let Granville see that my own bodyguard is sent to protect the secret."

" Very well, sir," assented the director, and took his departure.

Lumley-Gotham turned to his son. " Do you feel all right? " he inquired.

" Yes, father."

" Then I suppose I may eat mine," said the old man, and swallowed the tablet. " You may go now." The son bowed and left the apartment.

Another guard approached and announced, " Mrs. Granville wishes to speak to her father." But Granville answered promptly, " It cannot be permitted."

Lumley-Gotham sat in his chair, gazing before him. Such were the physician's orders —he must remain motionless for a certain period after every meal. Not even the greatest emergencies of state were permitted to intrude upon his mind. So it was an unprecedented thing when the guard came back and whispered once more to Granville. The Secretary of State ordered him away. But Lumley-Gotham turned his head quickly

—a motion strictly forbidden. "What's the matter?" he demanded.

"Nothing," Granville answered. "Do not disturb yourself, sir." To the guard he said, "She cannot see him."

"But she insists, sir," said the guard. "She will not be denied."

"If she makes any disturbance," was the answer, "arrest her immediately."

"Arrest your wife, sir?" stammered the guard.

"Such are my orders."

But these orders had come too late. An angry voice was heard at one side, causing Lumley-Gotham to start from his chair, and bringing to a sudden stop his processes of digestion. Helen Granville strode upon the scene, setting at defiance the levelled weapons of a couple of the guards.

"What does this mean?" cried the old man, in dismay; and Granville stepped forward, commanding, "Stop!"

But Helen came on. "Father, I wish to speak to you!"

"What do you want?" cried Lumley-Gotham, gazing first at his daughter, then at her husband.

" Father——"

" Stop ! " exclaimed Granville ; and then to the guards, " Seize her ! "

" Father ! " cried the girl, struggling desperately. " You must hear me ! "

" What does this mean—what is the matter? " quavered the old man.

A couple of the guards had grasped the woman's arms. " How dare you ! " she cried, stamping her foot with fury. " Father, bid these ruffians release me."

" Take her away," commanded Granville.

" But wait ! " cried the old man, wildly. " What does she want ? What is the matter ? "

" Mr. Lumley-Gotham," said the Secretary of State, " I warn you that you must not heed her. The matter is disturbing, and wholly unsuited to be brought to your attention. You know that you have just eaten, and you know the warnings of your physician. For an indiscretion like this you might pay with your life."

The master of the world quivered visibly. " Helen ! " he exclaimed. " How dare you disturb me ! How wicked of you to risk your father's life ! " And as she continued to shout to him, old Lumley-Gotham put his fingers to his ears, and fled from the scene of peril, followed by his crowd of trumpeters and guards.

So Helen ceased her struggles, and stood confronting her husband, white with anger. For a minute neither of them spoke; but at last she said, in a low voice, "You may command these men to set me free. I shall make no further resistance."

"I am glad you have come to your senses," was Granville's answer. He signalled to the guards to take their hands from her. "You should have known you could accomplish nothing," said he.

"I am not through," she answered.

He smiled. "You will try your mother next, I presume. Let me tell you this at the outset. You will not save Billy Kingdon's life. All you can do is to spread a scandal about yourself."

Helen's eyes blazed. "You consent to fight your wife with such weapons?"

"It is not a question of my consent. I might be the first to deny it, but how much heed would the world pay? Everyone knows that the young man loved you before your marriage; everyone knows that is the reason he ran away and became a common labourer. Now he returns, an engineer, the captain of the aeroplane—and I find you two together, planning to elope. What more will the world ask? What more *could* it ask?"

There was a pause. Helen answered, " I am only concerned to save his life. You have him in prison—at your mercy. Let me make this one thing clear to you : if you take his life, you make me your enemy. The fact that you are my husband will not deter me—and sooner or later I shall win my father to my side. All these years I have stood by and let you rule the world in your own way. But if you commit this crime I shall stand by no longer, I shall become your active opponent. You may think that you can afford to defy me—but I assure you the day will come when you will regret the step."

Granville faced the steady gaze of his wife, wondering a little at the new resolve he read there. But the issue of this duel was never to be known. At that moment they were interrupted by a blast of Lumley-Gotham's trumpets. The guards came in running, and immediately behind them came the old man, tottering, breathless with excitement. " Granville ! "

" What is it ? "

The owner of the world held out a copy of a newspaper in his trembling hand. " Look at this ! Look at this ! Radiumite again ! I declare I will not stand for it ! "

Granville took the paper. He read : " ' The Source of Radiumite ! New and astonishing discoveries by the Department of Inventions ! '

" We settled that," he remarked.

" Read on ! " cried the other. " Read it ! "

Granville read : " ' Professor Holcombe, of the Department of Inventions, announced to-night that he has discovered the original derivative of the radiumite emanations, and has succeeded in unlocking the key to the store-house of atomic energy. To a group of his fellow scientists, and a representative of the Universal Press Association, the eminent scientist exhibited a quart jar, hermetically sealed, containing a purplish gas which he has named X-radiumite. To quote the Professor's own account, its ionic constituents——' " Granville stopped. " What's the matter with all this? " he said. " I don't see anything wrong."

" Go on! " cried the other. " That second column—over there! "

The Secretary of State read at the place indicated : " ' The significance of this extraordinary feat may be appreciated when Professor Holcombe's statement is pondered, that in this single quart jar is contained an energy greater than any known upon earth. The sole difficulty is the impossibility of controlling this X-radiumite. It was produced in a vacuum; if by any chance the substance were to become mixed with air, the result would be more dreadful than a human mind can conceive. The jar is kept packed in cottonwool and is guarded by a laboratory assistant day and night. The Professor declared that if the jar were dropped the result would be the annihilation of all animal life upon the surface of the globe.' "

" Absurd! " exclaimed Granville.

But the old man was beside himself with alarm. " Do you hear what it says? If that jar were dropped—I should be killed! Think of such things being allowed! "

" But it can't be true ! "

" It is true !   Read on ! "

" ' This was conclusively shown,' read Granville, ' in the tragic death of the late Professor Clark, President of the Lumley-Gotham Foundation. Professor Clark, it will be recalled, was experimenting with a small quantity of radiumite—yet he was killed, together with everyone in his laboratory, only a small heap of dust being left where he had been standing.''

" Think of that ! " screamed Lumley-Gotham. " There would be nothing left of me but dust !   And what are they going to do with the stuff?   To signal to Mars ! "

Granville continued reading : " Professor Holcombe had hoped that it might be possible to use X-radiumite to reply to the signals which for the last ten years have been received from the inhabitants of the planet Mars. The Professor admitted, however, that his efforts were checked by the same difficulty which Clark and others found, that the radiumite emanations adhere closely to the earth. In the case of all previous experiments, it has been found impossible to drive the radiumite rays more than a quarter of a mile from the earth. Sufficient intensity of radiumite rays has been obtained to send them eight or ten thousand times around the earth, but they will not leave the ground for any distance.''

The reader stopped.

'' Did you ever hear such insanity in your life? '' demanded Lumley-Gotham.

Granville clenched his hands. '' We'll settle that,'' he said, and stepped to the wireless telephone apparatus. '' Department of Inventions. Police office. Hello. This is Granville. Special orders of Mr. Lumley-Gotham. Instruct your agents at the Foundation Laboratories to take charge of the place at once. Arrest Professor Holcombe and everyone in the building and hold them until further orders. Suppress all news of the procedure.'' Granville turned away. '' There,'' he said, '' that will do. And now, Mr. Lumley-Gotham, dismiss all further worry about the matter from your mind. I'll keep it in hand.''

'' Thank God! '' said Lumley-Gotham.

There was a pause. Then Helen advanced, chance having given her this fresh opportunity. '' Father——'' she began.

The old man started in alarm; and Granville sprang to his side. " I have already told you, Mr. Lumley-Gotham, that you must not heed her."

" Father, listen to me! "

" Remember your doctor's orders," insisted the other.

" Oh, dear me! What does this mean? " wailed the old man. " Can't I be spared such assaults from my own children? "

" If you take my advice," said Granville, " you will leave immediately." Turning to his wife, he added, " Are you resolved to inflict upon yourself the humiliation of an arrest? "

Lumley-Gotham himself saw his opportunity. He started to run away. But there came the sharp ringing of a bell, and a voice from the air : " Emergency wireless for Mr. Lumley-Gotham! "

" What's that? " cried the old man, in terror.

" I will see," said Granville, and stepping to a receiver, he diverted the message to himself. The others saw a look of sudden amazement come upon his face. " *What?* "

" What's the matter? " demanded Lumley-Gotham.

" Wait ! " exclaimed the other, his usually impassive face betraying emotion.

" What is it? " shouted Lumley-Gotham. " What are they saying to you? "

Granville turned from the 'phone. " The Professor has gone mad ! " he exclaimed.

" What? "

" He refuses to cease his investigations ! He's barricaded himself in his room, and declares he'll finish his work or smash the jar ! "

There was a moment of silence. All were staring at Granville.

" But what shall we do? " whispered the old man.

" The police are trying to get at him, but they are afraid of the explosion——"

" Tell them to stop ! " broke out Lumley-Gotham, frantically. " Call it off ! Make terms with him ! "

Granville turned to the 'phone. " Tell our agents to stop," he commanded. " Let him alone. Wait further orders."

He listened, and then responded : " They say the Professor won't trust them ! He won't make terms ! "

Lumley-Gotham began wringing his hands. "There it is!" he wailed. "Rebels! More rebels! Merciful providence, will there never be an end to my troubles? First the labour unions rebel! Then the engineers rebel! Then the women! Rebels, all rebels! And they want to kill me! My God, why was this laid upon me?" Suddenly his voice rose to a shriek: "Help! Help!"

Hearing his father's voice, Lumley-Gotham, junior, rushed into the room—in spite of all the regulations. "What's the matter?"

His father paid no attention to him, but stretched out his hands to the sky, as if addressing the mysterious power which had laid upon him the burden of life. "What have I done? What do you want me to do? Why did you put this curse upon me? Why couldn't you let me be a poor man, and sleep in a gutter—anywhere, so that I might sleep? Oh my God! my God!"

His cries had reached to the ball-room. His younger daughter, Eloise, had been standing at the entrance, awaiting the signal for her fancy dance; she came running towards her father demanding, "What has happened?"

" It's a professor gone crazy! He wants to blow us all into dust! "

" Why don't you do something? " shrieked the son.

" But what can I do? Granville, can't you tell me something? "

" You might consult Jessup," suggested Granville, having by this time recovered his usual blasé air.

" Yes! Jessup! " cried Lumley-Gotham. The son rushed off to the ball-room, shrieking, " Where's Jessup! Jessup! Jessup! "

Meantime the old man was pacing up and down the room, wringing his hands. " Oh, horrible! Horrible! The fate of a rich man! Why won't they let me be a labourer, and be let alone? "

The excitement had now spread to the other guests. Most of them dared not violate the law which made Lumley-Gotham's presence sacred; but the Lord Bishop came running, his episcopal robes streaming out behind him. " What's happened? What's this I hear about blowing us up? "

" I might have known that man would make trouble! " wailed Lumley-Gotham. " Why didn't you foresee it, Granville? "

Reginald Simpkins came next, wringing his hands and crying, " Save us! Where shall we go? " And then Mrs. Lumley-Gotham, hobbling upon her two-inch heels, and shrieking, " Murder! murder! "

Granville turned to the 'phone. " Hello! Any news yet? " There was a pause, while he listened. " Nothing yet."

" Oh, most horrible! " panted Lumley-Gotham himself.

" Let's go downstairs! " exclaimed Reggie.

" What good will that do? " cried Eloise.

The sedate Sarita Knickerbocker-Smythe came rushing from the ball-room, shouting, " Fire! Fire! " Following her came de Puyster, society reporter of the Universal Press Association, demanding, " Where is the fire? " He ran to one of the telephones, calling, " Hello! Universal Press Association. City department. This is de Puyster. I have a rumour that the Pleasure Palace is burning up. Get out an extra about it at once. I will verify the rumour if I can." He turned to the guests. " Please don't keep me waiting! I'm a reporter! I must have the news! Where is the fire? "

Mrs. Lumley-Gotham burst out, hysterically, " Can't somebody tell us what to do ? "

Lumley-Gotham seized his Secretary of State by the arm. " Think, think ! " he exclaimed. " I have always been able to depend upon you. Surely you can tell us ! "

Granville stood, deep in thought. " It just occurs to me; the paper stated that the rays do not go very far above the earth. So, if we went up in the aeroplane——"

There was a shout from the guests. " The aeroplane ! The very thing ! Up into the sky ! "

" But who can run the aeroplane ? " cried Lumley-Gotham.

There was a pause. Granville made no reply; but Helen stepped forward. " The captain of the aeroplane was here," she said.

" Where is he now ? " demanded her father.

" My husband knows," said Helen.

And so all turned upon Granville. " Where is he ? " And as the man remained silent, Helen cried loudly, " He knows where the man is ! You have but to give the order ! "

" Is that true ? " growled Lumley-Gotham.

There was a pause. Granville's reluctance

was obvious; but equally obvious was the demand from all the rest. " Bring him out! Where is he? What's the matter with you? "

So at last the Secretary of State turned to one of the guards. " Send for the man," he said. Meantime, he stepped to the 'phone; but only to report that there was no news.

All stood watching, breathless with terror —until suddenly an elevator shot into view, and Billy Kingdon stepped forth. " The captain of the aeroplane! " cried Helen.

There was a general shout from the guests. " On board! On board! "

One could scarcely have believed that these were the same people who a short while before had been moving with such stately dignity, with such acute consciousness of their social position and its requirements. The solemn Lord Bishop scurried like a schoolboy; nor heeded the fact that the poet and the society reporter were treading upon his episcopal train. The head butler shoved his mistress to one side, and leaped on board ahead of her. The stout Sarita grabbed the arm of Billy Kingdon, regardless of the fact that he was a member of the engineer caste and therefore a degraded inferior. Eloise Lumley-Gotham scrupled not to push her old father out of the way; indeed, in the general rush he might have been left behind altogether, had not his other daughter caught him by the arm and hurried him on board.

No one thought of the other guests who were in the ball-room. Billy Kingdon, of course, had no idea what was the situation— he only knew that for some mysterious reason he had been set free and ordered to make a flight in the air. He saw that Helen was on board the aeroplane, and that was all he cared about. He shut the doors of the machine, threw back the levers which controlled the moorings, and stepped into the conning-tower. There came the whirring of the huge propellers, and the machine began to slide along its launching-track.

At this moment was heard a terrified scream from the landing-stage. Lumley-Gotham, junior, had suddenly appeared, followed by Jessup, whom he had gone to seek. Both saw what had happened—they were left behind! The young heir of all the world rushed to the landing-stage, as if he would leap upon the outer platform of the machine; but already, with a whir as of a flock of a million birds, it was launched upon the air. Both the young heir of the world and his Director of Inventions were frantic with terror.

They rushed up and down, shrieking, " They have left us to die! The wretches! The villains! " And their cries reached the ball-room, from which the guests came pouring in a terrified throng.

Afar up in the air the aeroplane could be seen passing over the building, with a faint hum of machinery. " They've left me! " screamed Lumley-Gotham, junior. " Oh, what shall I do? What shall I do? " He tore at his collar, as if he were choking.

Higher and higher rose the Monarch of the Air, till it became a mere speck of light; and meantime the agitation of the guests increased. Then all at once every light in the apartment was extinguished; the next moment the room became filled with a vivid, blinding light. The guests, with their hands clasped to their heads, shrieked in agony, and collapsed upon the floor.

The light faded away, and there followed utter darkness, and a hush as of a tomb. Eleven people had gone up in the Monarch of the Air; and as that was the only machine allowed in the sky that night, those eleven were now the only human creatures left alive in all the world!

Six hours after the great explosion the Monarch of the Air came back to the Pleasure Palace. It had left the great structure ablaze with light and resounding with the strains of music. It returned in the faint light of dawn, to a building dark and silent as the tomb.

Ordinarily it was the custom to announce the arrival of one of the great ships of the upper air-lines by means of the wireless telephone; so a crew of men would be ready to handle the complicated machinery which broke the vessel's speed and made her fast to the landing-stage. But now the captain of the aeroplane signalled in vain; there came no response, nor any sign of life about the Pleasure Palace. He made his landing as best he could, and sprang out and opened the doors leading to the interior of the vessel.

The guests came timidly forth, and gazed about them in bewilderment at the scene of the festivities they had left. There was the roof-garden and the ball-room, the sumptuous decorations—everything as it had been; but nowhere was there a sound, nor a sign of a human being. Billy Kingdon sprang to the telephone and called, but there came no response. He ran to the elevator and signalled there, but no elevator appeared, nor was there any motion of the machinery.

Suddenly he noticed the temperature of the apartment; he had left it warm, even over-heated; but now it was chilly with the breeze of an April dawn. He turned to Helen Granville, who had joined him. They looked at each other, but could not bring themselves to speak what was in their minds.

Their eyes roamed about the room. Here and there on the floors Billy noticed little heaps of dust. "Look!" he whispered; and Helen caught his arm.

But they had no time for discussion. The rest of the party were clamouring about their troubles. Mrs. Lumley-Gotham commanded imperiously that Billy should find out what was the matter with the elevators. Old Lumley-Gotham, shivering, and with chattering teeth, demanded that his attendants be summoned to bring a coat. Where were his guards and his trumpeters? How preposterous that he should be neglected! Even more excited, if possible, was de Puyster, who ran from one telephone to the other, agonized because he had missed all the morning editions of the newspapers.

Billy tried to explain that he could do nothing; apparently there was no one to answer signals—no one to wait upon them, no one to rescue them.

" But what in the world are we to do? " cried Sarita.

" Surely somebody will answer! " insisted Eloise.

" Can't you go and send word? " cried the Bishop.

" Go where? " inquired Billy. " Send word to whom? "

" Call a messenger-boy! " cried Sarita.

" Send a telegram! " suggested the poet.

" The first problem," said Billy, " is to get down from this building. You must understand that we are a hundred stories in the air, and the elevators are not running."

" But how preposterous! " cried Mrs. Lumley-Gotham. " They will have to make them run! "

" If there has been an explosion of the

radiumite, then possibly there is nobody left to make them run.''

" But," cried the old lady, " send to the city! "

"Mother," put in Helen, "don't you understand? The people in the city may be dead, too."

" All the working people? " cried Eloise, in consternation.

" I'm afraid so."

" But how absurd! What in the world would we do? "

" There would be nobody to wait on us! " exclaimed Sarita.

" We should have nothing to eat! " added Reggie.

" There would be nobody to cook for us! " cried the Bishop.

" It's absurd! " Eloise declared. " It's not to be thought of! We should be like savages! "

Her mother burst out hysterically, " I won't have it, I won't have it! I will notify the government! " She turned to the reporter. " Mr. de Puyster, can't you get word to the newspapers about this? "

" I am trying to do it," wailed de Puyster.

" If I could only get someone to take my notes to the office! I have missed all the morning editions! "

Billy Kingdon sought to comfort him. " Can't you understand—there won't be any papers? "

The other looked dazed. " No papers? "

" Who would print them? "

" That is no business of mine! " responded de Puyster. " I represent the Universal Press Association, and we are under contract to furnish them the news, whether they print it or not." He began moving up and down in front of the elevators, pressing the buttons, and muttering, " I must get to the city! I must get to the city! "

After talking over the problem with Helen, Billy Kingdon declared that they would have to set about descending the stairs.

" But how preposterous! " cried Mrs. Lumley-Gotham, who had not walked a step in public for many years. " Can't we fly down in the aeroplane? "

" Yes, Mrs. Lumley-Gotham, but we'd have to land out in the country and walk back to the city."

" But couldn't we send for automobiles? "

E

" Couldn't we at least take the street cars? " insisted Eloise.

Billy waited for the truth to break into their minds. " I am sure," he said at last, " the simplest thing will be to walk downstairs. I will go alone, if you wish, and see what I can learn."

But they were not willing to be left without him; and so a strange pilgrimage began. What pen could tell the sighs, groans and lamentations which were expended in the course of it! People who had been kept in luxury, and had never had to lift a finger in their own behalf, whose costumes, manners and ideas were all selected for the purpose of expressing their inability to do anything for themselves—now suddenly found themselves obliged to descend ninety-nine successive flights of steps! Many times had the marble staircases of the Pleasure Palace been pictured in the newspapers; but what diabolical contrivances they seemed, when one had to descend them all on foot!

One by one the members of this party kicked off their high-heeled slippers. Mrs. Lumley-Gotham, gasping for air, tore loose her corsage of diamonds—and after carrying

it a few flights farther she flung it to the floor.
Tuttle, the head butler, red-faced and portly,
picked it up and carried it an additional
distance—and then dropped it in turn.
Other members of the party threw away
bracelets and arm-rings containing jewels without price—because these objects interfered
with their clinging to the balustrade and lean-
ing their weight upon it. His Grace, the
Lord Bishop of Harlem, stripped off one after
another of his robes of office; finally, when
his pudgy limbs would no longer support him,
he climbed upon the balustrade, a fat and
sputtering object, and began to slide!
Flight after flight, shouting to the rest to
keep out of his way—and without the slightest
regard for the ecclesiastical proprieties!

There was a strange sight to be seen upon
the ground floor of the Pleasure Palace, soon
after sunrise on that April morning. Down
the staircase, made of snow-white marble,
with carvings upon which great artists had
spent lifetimes—down this staircase a pro-
cession of tattered and tottering creatures
made their appearance one by one. First
came Reginald Simpkins, the poet, who was
the lightest of all of them, and had looked out

for no one but himself. Then came Eloise and Sarita, practically barefoot, having worn out their diaphanous silk stockings on the way. Next came de Puyster, with barely enough energy to struggle to the telephone, and to wring his hands in despair over the first afternoon edition.

Then came His Grace, the Lord Bishop of Harlem—or rather came the voice of His Grace: " Mercy, mercy! Help! What shall I do? Is that the bottom? "

Again he shouted, until Eloise answered, " Yes, you fool! "

" Heaven be praised! " Then came a shriek, " Clear the way! I'm coming! " He came with violence, and landed on the floor, close to where the others were lying.

Next came Mrs. Lumley-Gotham, moaning, " Let me die in peace! " It would be inconsiderate to describe the extent to which the great lady had disrobed during this ordeal. Let the sensitive reader avert his eyes while we mention that she was borne, half in the arms of the captain of the aeroplane, and half in the arms of the head butler, who answered her protests as to the number of stairs by the impertinent remark that she had built them herself. Outraged by this, the Lord Bishop got up and tried to help her; but he had slid down so many circular balustrades that he was dizzy, and staggered like a drunken man, colliding with Helen Granville, who arrived with her father on her arm.

Billy Kingdon hurried out to see if it was possible to get help. He did not return, and after half an hour or so, Helen bestirred herself. "We must get some food," she said, and looked about for the head butler. "Tuttle, is there nothing to drink near?"

The man addressed was sprawled upon a sofa, and did not manifest that alacrity which was second nature to a member of the upper servant caste. "I don't know, ma'am," he answered.

"Isn't it your place to know?" asked the Bishop.

"No, it ain't," was the reply.

"Well, get up and look!" insisted Helen. "These people must have help."

"I'm just as tired as the rest," said Tuttle; but he got up and shambled off.

Once more the company relapsed into silence, and for some minutes there was no sound but moans of despair. At last Tuttle returned, bearing half a dozen bottles of champagne in his arms. "I foun' somethin' a' right!" he repeated. "A' you wan'!"

"Tuttle!" cried Mrs. Lumley-Gotham, with what was meant to be crushing severity.

His reply was to hold out a bottle to her. "How're y', lady? Have one wiz me?"

It was Reginald Simpkins who sprang to protect the Mistress of Society. "You infernal scoundrel!" he exclaimed.

Tuttle turned upon him with a snort. "What do you mean?"

"Why, Tuttle!" gasped Reggie, with a sudden falling of the voice.

"You young puppy!" muttered the other.

It was the Lord Bishop's turn to interpose. "Tuttle!" he said, gravely. "Tuttle! You forget your place!"

The other burst into a noisy laugh. "My place? What *is* my place?"

The Bishop stared at him. "Why, what do you mean?"

"What do I mean, hey? You've lorded it over me in your time, old boy—but d'ye think you can do it still? Who's the man in this crowd now?"

Mrs. Lumley-Gotham forgot her exhaustion,

so great was her wrath. She rose to her feet, demanding : " Do you know whose house this is ? "

The remark appealed to the sense of humour of the head butler. " It's yours, ma'am," he retorted. " But I don't see as it'll do you much good."

" Ungrateful wretch ! " exclaimed the great lady. " You are discharged from my service ! "

" Well, ma'am, I wasn't anxious to wait on you." And Tuttle proceeded to turn one of the bottles up to his mouth.

" Monster ! " cried Mrs. Lumley-Gotham. " Leave my house this instant ! "

" Ho, ho, ho ! " cried the other. " Anybody want to put me out ? Send for the police, maybe ! "

The great lady turned to her husband. " Mr. Lumley-Gotham, you are the head of this household. Order that villain away ! "

But Lumley-Gotham, who was stretched out upon one of the steps of the staircase, made no move. " My dear," he said, in his quavering voice, " I've no quarrel with him."

" You bet ! " said Tuttle, with a grin.

"That's the way to talk to me! Here, old boy, have a drink."

Lumley-Gotham hesitated a moment, then sat up and stretched out his hands. Seizing the bottle, he turned it up over his mouth, while his wife stood staring in helpless fury.

Tuttle began strutting up and down the apartment. "I'm the boss of this crowd now! I've got the key to the wine cellar, and anybody that wants it comes to me!" But at this moment Granville appeared in the doorway and strode towards him. "Tuttle!" he said. "Give me that key."

"What?" cried Tuttle, blustering.

"Give me that key!"

And the head butler hesitated but a moment. "Yes, sir," he said, and gave up the key.

"Now get out!" exclaimed Granville.

Tuttle slunk off; and so ended the first labour rebellion.

Everyone turned to the Secretary of State as their new deliverer.

"Have you had any news?" asked Sarita.

"News?" answered Granville. "Who is there to make news?"

" Surely there may be people elsewhere ! "

" It is possible. But how can we find out? "

" Can't we wireless? " cried Eloise.

" Do you know how to work a wireless instrument? "

A gleam of hope came to Sarita. " My yacht is down at the dock. Couldn't we take that? "

Granville shrugged his shoulders. " If you know how to run it."

"Good heavens ! " exclaimed Mrs. Lumley-Gotham. " We can't really do anything ! "

Granville laughed. " Yes, my lady ! So it seems ! The game is up. Someone has dumped the chessboard." And with a gesture of despair he turned and strode from the room.

The silence was broken by the Lord Bishop. " Sarita," he whispered, " there are no more cooks in the world ! "

They gazed at each other. " We'll have to eat cold food ! " murmured the Bishop. And then, after another silence, " Maybe we won't have any food at all ! "

" No more quail in aspic ! " whispered Sarita.

"No more lobster salad!" sighed the Bishop. "No more paté de foie gras!"

Then came the voice of Eloise. "No more theatre parties!"

".My God!" cried Reginald Simpkins. "No more tailors!" He looked about him, dazed. "Why, I'll have to wear ready-made clothing!" Then, his voice breaking, "I'll have nobody to print my poems!"

"Stop!" cried Sarita. "I can't bear this!"

There was a silence. Finally the Bishop pulled at her sleeve. "Sarita," he whispered, "do you suppose those deviled skylarks' livers are all ruined?"

"Oh, Your Grace, you break my heart!"

The voice of Lumley-Gotham himself was heard, calling feebly for a brandy and soda. Then came his wife's voice: "I'm so cold! Can't somebody get me a wrap?"

Helen rose. "Here, mother," she said, "take this shawl." Then, turning to Reginald, "Can't you find something for mother to put on?"

"I don't know where anything is," answered the poet.

"But can't you look?"

" For goodness sake," cried Eloise, " why doesn't somebody turn on the heat? "

" I suppose the furnaces are out," was Sarita's suggestion.

" Furnaces out? " cried Mrs. Lumley-Gotham. " But that's preposterous! In the middle of April? Send for the major-domo! Send—oh, I forgot! "

Said the Bishop addressing the company : " Is there anybody who knows how to run a furnace? "

Silence followed. Apparently there was nobody. " We'll freeze to death! " wailed Mrs. Lumley-Gotham.

" We must surely have a fire," said Helen, moving about impatiently.

" How does one start a fire? " inquired Eloise.

Reginald Simpkins got up. " You have to find something that will burn," he said.

The Lord Bishop arose also. " Something that's wood, I believe." He began examining one of the gold chairs. " Do you suppose there is any wood in this? They sometimes make chairs of wood, don't they? "

" Seems to me I have read about it," said Reggie.

"That settee is wood," declared Helen. "Burn that."

"What?" cried Mrs. Lumley-Gotham, in horror. "That's an antique!"

"It's real Louis Quinze!" added Eloise. "Cost thirty-seven thousand dollars!"

"I don't care!" came the peevish voice of Lumley-Gotham himself. "Burn it, and be damned!"

"All right," said Reggie. He dragged the settee out to the centre of the floor and stood looking at it. "Now," he exclaimed, "let it burn!"

"You have to break it up first," said Helen.

"Of course," exclaimed the Bishop, with scorn for the poet's stupidity. "Get out of the way!" And lifting one end of the settee, he flung it violently upon the ground. When that had no effect, he upset it and dragged it half-way across the room.

"Here!" cried Reggie. "You pull one way and I'll pull the other."

They exerted themselves until they were red in the face but still the obstinate settee showed no signs of parting. "Get out of the way! Let me show you!" exclaimed the

Bishop, and gave the obstacle several violent kicks. Then, grunting at it in a rage, he seized one end and beat it again and again upon the floor. Suddenly he gave a cry of triumph; he had managed to break off one leg. "Now! I'm getting it!" he proclaimed.

"But that won't do much good," declared Sarita; "it has to be split up."

"We ought to have an axe," said Helen.

"An axe?" echoed Reggie. "Where in the world would we find an axe?"

"Let's find Tuttle," suggested the Bishop. "He ought to know."

"I have a knife," put in the poet; "perhaps that will do." He produced his tiny gold-handled pocket-knife.

"No, no!" exclaimed the Bishop. "I am getting along all right now. Just give me a little time." He began to pound the unfortunate antique until he broke off the rest of the legs and got the back separated from the seat. "Now it will burn," he said. "But we need something to start the fire."

Reggie produced a jewelled case from his pocket. "Here are matches," he said.

"We must have some paper," suggested

the Bishop. He gazed about the room. " Something that will burn quickly."

Helen pointed to one of the doorways of the entrance hall. " Try that tapestry."

" What? " shouted Mrs. Lumley-Gotham. " That is Flemish tapestry! It cost nearly two hundred thousand dollars! "

" Burn it! " cried the voice of Lumley-Gotham himself.

They dragged the priceless art work from the wall, and Reggie and the Bishop got hold of opposite ends and pulled and tore at it until they had it in strips. Then they bundled it up, and Reggie struck a match and sought to ignite it. But the match had no effect. They tried one match after another, but the tapestry would not burn.

" The stuff is no good! " Reggie exclaimed.

" What can be the matter? " demanded Sarita.

" Fools! " exclaimed Eloise. " None of the hangings in the house will burn. They made them fireproof! "

Again there was silence; until suddenly the poet made a dash at the Bishop and seized what was left of his episcopal robes. " Is this fireproof? "

" No, no! Stop! " protested the Bishop.

" Give it to me! " raged the poet.

" You villain! "

But Mrs. Lumley-Gotham stamped her foot. " Let him have it this instant! "

So the Bishop submitted, and Reggie tore the robe into strips. He piled a chair-leg on top of it, and struck another match and started a feeble flame. Everybody crowded about, shivering and trying to warm their fingers. They crowded so close that the front ones were nearly driven into the fire. It was with difficulty that Helen managed to persuade them to make room for her mother and father, who were the oldest and most helpless.

Mrs. Lumley-Gotham was distressed about her diamond corsage which had been left upon the stairs. Helen had to repeat several times that there was not the least danger of anyone's stealing it; nobody wanted diamonds— diamonds no longer had value. This suggested a new idea to them—the most horrible yet. There was no more money in the world! None of them was worth anything!

They broke into hysterical laughter as they realized this.

" No more banks! " gasped the Bishop.

" No more Wall Street ! " added Sarita.

So they went on—no more this, no more that; until suddenly Lumley-Gotham himself, who had been crouching by the fire, leaped to his feet with a startled ejaculation : " I'm free ! " They thought the old man had gone out of his mind—and really, he looked like a maniac, waving his arms and laughing deliriously, " I'm free ! Free ! "

" What do you mean? " cried his wife, in amazement.

" I've got rid of it ! All of it ! All of it ! "

" Of what? "

" My money ! I won't have to sign any more cheques ! I won't have to do any more business ! "

" Father ! " cried Eloise, horrified at his blasphemy.

" It's true ! It's true ! People won't bother me any more ! They won't write about me ! They won't throw bombs at me ! They'll let me alone, and I can do what I please—I can be happy ! " He sank into his chair and buried his face in his hands, sobbing with the excess of his relief. " Free ! Free ! "

" Oh, this is terrible ! " cried Mrs. Lumley-Gotham.

" Why ! " exclaimed Sarita. " It's like a bad joke by some Socialist ! "

" It's like a nightmare ! " declared Eloise.

" It's an outrage ! " continued Sarita. " And upon persons of our station ! Why, we are no better than common labouring people ! "

" There should at least have been a few more servants left ! " ventured Reggie.

St. Erskine Granville had appeared in the doorway of the room, and he answered this remark. " Do you suppose the servants would have waited on you? I found Tuttle just now on his way here with one of your antique battle-axes." Then, at their chorus of horror, he laughed. " The mob is up ! The forces of revolution are unchained ! The red flag is in our streets ! "

The Bishop stared at him in consternation.

" Sir, I believe you have been drinking." And this was hardly a miracle of divination—for Granville had an open bottle of whisky in either hand. The company was aghast ; never before had this man of iron been known to share in human frailty.

" His nerves are unstrung by this dreadful affair," said the Bishop, apologetically.

But the other laughed more loudly. " What do you think of your God? He sleeps, perchance, and dreams ill? Or has someone knocked his elbow? Or is he drunk, like me? "

" Mr. Granville, this is blasphemy! "

" The wine cellar is open," laughed the other. " Help yourself, and see what *you* say! "

" Granville," remarked Mrs. Lumley-Gotham, haughtily, " I should think that in a time of distress like this——"

" What, my lady! " cried the other. " Are we still going to be moral? Are we going to build all over again? Tell me, oh, brothers to the faithful ants! " He paused for an answer, but none came. " My spirit mounts," he laughed—" upon the wings of——" He consulted the label on the bottles in order to make sure. " Of Royal Irish Whisky! I behold the answer to the riddle—writ so large that we can read it with shut eyes! See the distant suns in their courses—shattered and whirled into flame! See the planets—dried up and dark—forgotten for ever! Or look beneath your feet, at the ant-hill you trample! Above, below, everywhere—life! Life that cries out to be! Life that says, ' Struggle, suffer! ' That bids me keep sober when I wish to be drunk! Ha, ha, ha! ''

The company sat terrified at his outburst, scarcely a word of which they were able to understand. Their startled faces moved him to renewed laughter. '' A row of death's heads at my feast. Cheer up, friends—to-day we jest with the gods! ''

'' This is horrible! '' cried Sarita. '' Have you no sense of decency left? ''

'' Decency, lady? That was the law of the game. But the game is over! ''

'' Sir, '' she answered, '' you will be ashamed of yourself. ''

'' I never believed in the game, '' he continued, '' but there was no other, so I played it. It amused me to play it better than the others; to watch their struggle, to read their minds and match their futile moves. But now—where are the pieces? The board has been dumped. ''

At this moment his wife stepped forward. '' Mr. Granville, '' she said, '' permit me to suggest that if you have nothing better to say to us, you might go and drink by yourself."

" My virgin wife ! " he exclaimed, and caught her by the wrist, exclaiming : " Come quaff a flagon with me ! "

She drew away, indignantly; but he held her fast. There began a physical struggle between them; but suddenly came the sound of an automobile, heard through the doorway. Lumley-Gotham heard it first, and started to his feet, crying, " What's that? "

" Someone alive ! " exclaimed the Bishop, and ran towards the door. But before he reached it a cheery voice rang out : " Hello ! "

" Billy ! " exclaimed Helen.

Her husband still held her by the wrist, and this was the sight that confronted Billy when he appeared before them. For a moment all stood as in a tableau; then Granville broke into laughter. " There is something to live for after all ! "

Billy looked at him, and then at the others. " What is the matter? " he asked. As the meaning of the thing dawned upon him, he remarked : " So soon, Granville? "

Helen got her arm free and moved towards Billy. " You have been to the city? "

He nodded, and they crowded about him in excitement. "What did you find? Tell us!"

"The same as here," he said—"nothing at all."

"No people?" cried Mrs. Lumley-Gotham.

"Not a soul."

"The whole city deserted?"

"Dead! You drive down Broadway—it's like a string of graveyards. There are cars, cabs, motors—not a soul in them. Little piles of dust on the sidewalk—piles in the shops—piles in the cars! But not a sound! Not a fly alive! You can motor on the sidewalks as fast as you please—there's no speed limit, no police." He paused and shrugged his shoulders. "But, somehow, it isn't as much fun as it used to be."

"Oh, horrible!" cried Sarita.

"Is everything else all right?" demanded Helen.

"Everything," he answered. "Food, drink, clothing, all there. But you have to go and get it. You can't pay anyone to bring it to you."

"It's outrageous!" cried the Mistress of Society.

"Why, Mrs. Lumley-Gotham!" said Billy, laughing in spite of himself. "What's the matter? You owned half the country—and now you can have the other half! You cried for the earth, and you've got it. Stuff your pockets with it—wrap your arms about it!"

"Billy!" exclaimed Helen, reproachfully.

"All right, my dear," he laughed. "I won't rub it in." He paused and looked around him. "Have you people any idea what you are going to do?" There was a silence. "Apparently not," he went on. "I suppose you are going on living—that's easiest. So I've brought you some tinned foods."

"Good!" exclaimed the Bishop. With Reggie at his heels, he started towards the feast.

But Billy checked him. "Just a minute, please. I've something else to say. We're under a new regime now, you understand—we begin the year one this morning. The sacred rights of property are abolished. I observe that the conventions are also dead—Mr. Reginald Simpkins wears evening dress in the morning, and His Grace, the Lord

Bishop, appears in his shirt-sleeves. So I, too, will break a few rules. I suppose most of you know already that I have loved Helen for many years."

Helen started; but he went on relentlessly, in spite of her protest. " I loved her before she was forced to marry. A ' marriage of state,' you called it—that was the way of your world. You drove me off with a threat of death; but last night I came back, meaning to take her with me—in spite of your world and all its laws. Now that world is gone— its laws are dead. So I shan't take her very far. But get this matter clear—her name from now on is Helen Kingdon, and not Helen Granville." And Billy turned towards the girl and held out his hand to her. " My love! "

Helen stood motionless, dazed by the suddenness of all this. " Come, dearest," he said, quietly. " We have loved each other truly, and we have waited long. There is no reason to wait any longer. You love me? "

She answered, gravely, " Yes, I love you."

At which her mother sprang forward with a horrified cry : " Helen! "

"I am sorry, Mrs. Lumley-Gotham," interposed Billy. "This is a matter between Helen and myself."

"Young man," said Granville, "I think I also have a share in it."

"Granville," said the young engineer, "you are drunk. You had better take my advice and wait. You will need your sober wits to handle such a matter."

"Billy," warned Helen, "don't provoke him."

"Really, my dear boy," continued the Secretary of State, "what I say may sound painfully melodramatic; but have you thought that this action may cost you your life?"

Billy stood watching him for a moment, and then began to laugh. "I wondered if you would take that line. A man of your brains at least should realize the change."

"What do you mean?"

"Last night you had nothing to do but telephone to the police and have me removed. But now see—if I am to die, you have to do the killing, the vulgar, brutal killing; think of that! You have to aim a weapon, or you have to take a knife in your hands and stab me!" He was eyeing Granville, and noted his uneasy look. "Horrible! Don't you see?"

"Billy," pleaded Helen, "do let us be sensible."

"Sensible, my dear? By all means! Granville is a gentleman; he knows all the rules of the game of intrigue—he made his early reputation at it. Perhaps we shall fight a duel! Wouldn't it be picturesque?"

Here Billy turned to the company. "Please understand me—from now on, this is my wife. We have selected for our honeymoon the bridal suite of the Consolidated Hotel, which occupies Broadway from 34th to 42nd streets. The warehouses of the Amalgamated Groceries Company are nearby —we shall find that a matter of importance. Helen and I have no desire to impose our ways on others; we leave you all the rest of the city. On the other hand, we don't wish to be snobbish—we shall be glad to extend any assistance to fellow-beings in distress. But anyone who joins our party must understand that the ancient right of being a parasite is at an end, and that everyone must do his share of all the work. And that is all—except that you will find an abundance of motors in the garage of the Pleasure Palace, and some tinned food and can-openers on the steps outside."

With these words he took Helen's hand in his. " Come, Helen! My wife! "

When it came to a show-down, of course, it was impossible for Billy and Helen to go alone. How could Mrs. Lumley-Gotham get along without them? Horrified as she was at their unconventional action, she came hobbling behind them insisting that they could not elope without a mother-in-law. And Lumley-Gotham himself was equally sure they needed a father-in-law. The Lord Bishop insisted that they needed the assistance of the church. De Puyster was determined that the press should be represented. In the end, the eloping young couple were accompanied by everyone except Tuttle, who was too drunk to walk.

The gigantic structure known as the Consolidated Hotel was a whole city in itself —a city now desolate and silent and cold. The new guests entered the palatial lobby, with its marble columns and decorations of gold. But no uniformed attendants rushed forward to welcome them; no smiling clerk stood behind the register with pen out-stretched. They sank into the velvet arm-chairs and couches, exhausted.

Some of them were cold and wanted blankets; but they realized that there were three flights of stairs to be ascended to the nearest bedrooms. The Lord Bishop wanted a drink; but the automatic bootlegging apparatus would no longer work, and it was a quarter of a mile to the nearest drug store. The pantries of the hotel were far in the base-ment, and it took quite a search on Billy's part before the simplest meal could be got ready. This once, he said, he and Helen would carry the food for the rest; but there-after they would have to do their own foraging.

So, after a few days of agonizing and lamenting, one might have seen these fastidious members of the best society camp-ing out in the servants' room below stairs, handy to the store-rooms and the kitchen. In the last-named place the wonderful electric cooking apparatus was useless; but Billy found an old stove in an antique shop, and this he set up so that they need no longer live upon cold food. Fortunately there was still running water, and food enough in the store-rooms of the Amalgamated Groceries Company to have fed them for thousands of years. There were inexhaustible supplies of clothing; the only drawback was that whatever one wanted, one had to go and hunt for it.

The dishes, for instance; when a dozen people sat down to a meal, it was incredible how many soiled dishes were left! They tried the plan of throwing them away; but the mere labour of throwing them was a burden, and pretty soon all the passages about the kitchen were filled up with piles of broken dishes. And there was Helen Granville, going about everywhere, lynx-eyed and tireless, making rules and insisting that everyone should obey them; and Billy Kingdon, backing her up with the threat that anyone who refused to obey would be driven out into the cold world to shift for himself!

Picture the aristocracy after a month, when their domestic arrangements had got somewhat ordered. Eloise Lumley-Gotham, younger daughter of the richest man in the world, wore a dirty silk ball-gown with the train torn off—for she had been too busy and tired to get anything else. She was seated by the kitchen table, peeling potatoes; and beside her was Sarita Knickerbocker-Smythe, heiress of the coal trust, wearing a ragged striped sweater, her hair towsled and her face and hands red from washing dishes.

" Oh, my Lord! " she grumbled. " How I hate peeling potatoes! "

" I can't see why we don't cook them in their skins," said Eloise.

" And fancy Reggie! " exclaimed Sarita. " Having the impudence to ask for them hash-browned! What does he take us for? "

Said Eloise, " He'll be wanting potato-salad with mayonnaise the next thing! He seems to think I've nothing better to do than to stick parsley on his food."

" It's the Bishop always egging him on," said the other. " I suppose they think when they've kept the kitchen fire going for half an hour they've earned the right to growl at everybody else in the place."

Then Reginald Simpkins, the poet, put in appearance, struggling along under the burden of a scuttle half-filled with coal. He set it down in the middle of the floor, and stood mopping his forehead, panting, " Oh, dear me! Those stairs get longer every day! "

"Yes, no doubt," sneered Sarita. "Why don't you learn to run the elevator?"

Eloise was peering into the coal-scuttle. "What's that? You call that a scuttle of coal?"

"What's the matter with it?"

"You go down and fill that scuttle, or I'll tell Billy about it this very day!"

"Oh, go to the devil!" exclaimed the poet.

Eloise surveyed him with infinite scorn. "And to think that a month ago you were begging me to marry you! You were calling me an angel!"

"Well," said Reggie, "you are a fallen angel!"

He approached the stove and began examining the contents of a steaming saucepan which sat at one side. "Um!" he muttered. "What's this?"

But at the same moment Mrs. Lumley-Gotham appeared in the doorway. "Reggie! Haven't I told you to keep away from that stove?"

Truly amazing was the change in the Mistress of Society. She was now the Mistress of the Kitchen, and took her work seriously. Espying a coat upon the table, she pounced upon it, crying, " Haven't I told you to keep your clothes out of the kitchen? "

" I didn't put it there," insisted the poet.

" Didn't I see you with it just now? "

" But I tell you——"

The unhappy youth got no further, for Mrs. Lumley-Gotham seized the frying-pan from the stove and swung it over her head. " Go and empty that garbage," she cried, " and don't let me hear from you until supper is ready." Then hearing her daughter's laughter she turned with the sharp command, " Go in and set the table! " After which the great lady sat down and wiped her face with her apron. " Oh, dear me! Dear me! Why can't people live on cold canned food? "

Said Sarita, " Why can't they eat rice and things that don't have to be peeled? That's what I want to know! "

" I should think," said the other, " they would try to spare me a little. With all the troubles I have on my hands! "

She was bidding for more sympathy; but the other's supply appeared to be exhausted. " So far as I can see," declared Sarita, " your troubles are mostly of your own making."

And forthwith there began an argument.

It was one instalment of a dispute which had been raging for a month—ever since that speech which Billy Kingdon had made at the Pleasure Palace. It was all very well to say that Helen's marriage to Granville was annulled, and that she was now Mrs. Kingdon; but that did not make it true in the eyes of mothers and sisters and bishops and newspaper reporters!

No sooner had the party reached the hotel than Mrs. Lumley-Gotham took Helen aside, and poured out her agony of spirit. Never before had a daughter of the line of Lumley-Gotham given cause for scandal! Helen was made to realize that the carrying out of Billy's plan would cause more distress than she could bear to inflict; and so in the end she went to Billy, and forced him to agree to the postponement of the question for a month.

Ever since which time the problem had been the theme of all discussions in the little community. Reggie and Eloise came to blows over it during dish-washing; and Sarita and Mrs. Lumley-Gotham argued about it all day long.

" You could put an end to the whole dispute so easily if you chose to! " cried Sarita.

"So easily!" echoed the other. "By letting my daughter live with a man she's not married to!"

"It wouldn't be the first time that happened among your guests," was the sarcastic reply.

"But with her lawful husband in the house!" cried Mrs. Lumley-Gotham.

"That's the safest way to arrange it, they tell me," retorted Sarita.

"And he knowing it! Everybody knowing it!"

"We used to say," Sarita reminded her, "that nothing mattered if it didn't get into the newspapers."

"Sarita, I can't understand you—such levity!"

"My dear woman, you must realize it—you've got to make up your mind sooner or later."

"I know! I know!" wailed Mrs. Lumley-Gotham, suddenly threatening tears.

"The month is up to-day," persisted the other. "And what have you to say to Billy and Helen?"

"I'm simply heart-broken!" exclaimed the great lady. "My family name dragged in the mire! Why——"

At this moment Eloise appeared in the doorway. "My God! Are you people at that again!"

Sarita paid no attention to her. "If you'd let Billy kick Granville out, that would settle it."

"Has anybody seen Granville to-day?" demanded Eloise.

"He stopped by this morning," said her mother.

"Drunk, as usual?" asked the girl.

"Why should he continue to come here?" demanded Sarita. "Isn't it perfectly clear that it's for nothing but to stir up strife? To distress Helen and you——"

Mrs. Lumley-Gotham interrupted suddenly. "Hush! Here comes the Bishop. Don't let him hear us! I'm so ashamed!"

Behold now the entrance of His Grace, the Lord Bishop of Harlem. You might have had to look twice to make sure of his identity —this rosy-faced old gentleman, clad in blue overalls and suspenders, carrying a huge armful of broken-up furniture. He staggered over to the stove and dropped it, and then stood wiping his forehead, gasping, "Goodness me, goodness me! This business of chopping furniture for kindling is exceedingly exhausting ! "

" No doubt," said Sarita, unsympathetically.

" They seem to have put the stuff together so tightly ! Do you know, I've half a mind to try the trees in Bryant Park."

Mrs. Lumley-Gotham's answer was to pick up one of the sticks and measure it on the range. " How do you expect me to burn that thing? " she demanded.

The man stood staring in dismay. " Oh, dear me ! "

" Take those long ones away and chop them ! " cried the other.

" I'll bring my axe up here," he suggested, timidly.

" And chop them on my hearth? "

He stood scratching his head and looking puzzled. " Maybe you'll find some other use for the long ones."

" For potato mashers? " inquired Sarita, sarcastically ; crushed by which cruel retort, the Bishop gathered up his firewood and carried it off, groaning.

Supper was nearly ready when Mr. Harold de Puyster made his entrance. He alone, of all the members of the little community, had preserved immaculate and inerrant the costume he had worn on the night of the opening ceremonies at the Pleasure Palace. He stood now in the doorway, and made an elaborate bow. " Good evening, ladies."

" Good evening," said Sarita, with more gentleness than she had displayed towards the others.

De Puyster took out a notebook. " I beg pardon," he said. " Is this Mrs. Viviana Athelstan de Smithkins Lumley-Gotham? Could you spare me the time for a brief interview to-day? "

The lady addressed was carrying the potatoes to the stove. " No time for interviews now, de Puyster."

" Oh, I'm so sorry ! " he exclaimed. " It's really a matter of great importance. The office has a rumour that there is to be a reconciliation in the Granville family. Can you tell me——"

Mrs. Lumley-Gotham pushed past him, exclaiming, " Run along, de Puyster."

" Alas ! " said the other, and made his way to the telephone system, through which in the old days the orders to the kitchen had been transmitted. " Hello, central. Give me the

Universal Press Association. Hello! Hello! The 'phone's out of order again! And I'll miss the third afternoon edition!"

He wandered off disconsolately, while Sarita shook her head. "Poor de Puyster!" she said. "I wonder if he'll ever get over the habit?"

Her painful thoughts were interrupted by the sound of cheerful whistling, heralding the arrival of Lumley-Gotham himself. You should have seen him come in—wearing a grocer's apron, and carrying an armful of canned goods! The richest man in the world was as old as he had ever been in his life, but he looked thirty years younger, and as happy as a schoolboy.

"Well, ladies!" he exclaimed, and set the goods on the table, and took from his pocket a list. "Will you see if these are all right?" he said, addressing his wife. "Sixteen quarts of peas, twelve tins of salmon, five pounds of crackers, and three bars of soap. The dried peaches I'll get this afternoon—the ones at the Amalgamated Grocery Company's seem to be spoiling."

The old gentleman turned to Sarita. "Do you know," he exclaimed, "I'm getting to be quite an expert chauffeur. I haven't had a collision to-day! And, oh, by the way, did you hear the story about the Bishop?"

"No," said Sarita. "What?"

"He went into a drug store to get a vanilla soda, and he hit on the castor oil. And now he's brushing up his Latin so he can read the labels!"

Mrs. Lumley-Gotham went out for a moment, and Sarita took the occasion to broach to Lumley-Gotham himself the subject which lay heaviest upon her mind. "About this business of Billy and Helen——" she began.

"Now, for heaven's sake, Sarita," the other interrupted, with signs of intense agitation, "don't try to drag me into that affair!"

"But the question has got to be settled some time——"

"I know, I know! But not by me!"

"Isn't Helen your daughter?"

"They told me she was," he answered, cautiously.

"You are the head of the house," persisted Sarita, without heeding this bad taste. "Consequently——"

" I don't want to be head of anything! " he exclaimed.

" But the responsibility of it——"

" I won't have it—I won't have anything to do with it! I'm not rich any more, and they've no right to bother me."

" But you are a man of the world, and you understand practical affairs. You could make your wife listen to reason——"

At which moment Mrs. Lumley-Gotham entered the room. " Sarita Knickerbocker-Smythe! He's never been able to do anything of the sort! "

The old man started in alarm. " Now, my dear——" he began.

" I tell you," exclaimed his wife, " marriage is marriage. And it is a sacred thing——"

" Oh, my goodness! " exclaimed Reggie, appearing in the doorway. " They're at it again! "

" Have you helped set the supper table? " cried Mrs. Lumley-Gotham, turning upon him. " Don't you see that supper's nearly ready? "

" Eloise says she has a headache," objected Reggie. " She won't work any more."

" Eloise! Eloise! " the old lady shouted,

in sudden passion. "You get up this instant and set that table! I tell you I've stood all the nonsense from you I will. If I hear of your shirking your work again you'll get not a bite of supper."

"I tell you, mother, I'm ill!" pleaded the girl from the other room.

"I tell you you're lazy!" was the furious reply. "You were never any good from the day you were born. You're a drone, an idler, a parasite! You want to lie around and enjoy yourself while other people work for you. I'm ashamed of myself for the way I brought you up!"

"W-well," sobbed Eloise, "the dishes are so heavy!"

Helen entered at this moment, and took up the burden of peacemaker. "Never mind," she said to the sobbing Eloise, "I'll help you get the table set!"

Helen wore the uniform of a trained nurse, and somehow had managed to find time to keep herself looking neat.

"My God!" exclaimed Mrs. Lumley-Gotham, "how I wish we had a few more Helens in this place!"

"Thanks, awfully!" remarked Sarita,

sarcastically. "Any fault to find with those potatoes, ma'am?"

"Now, ladies, ladies!" interposed old Lumley-Gotham, pleadingly. "Why make our burdens harder than they are? A little kindness goes such a long way."

"It has to, in this crowd!" snapped Sarita.

Billy Kingdon came in, clad in a flannel shirt and overalls, grimy with coal-dust. He had put in a hard day's work—for he was looking ahead, and imagining the winter, with an insufficient supply of coal in their quarters. "We've hauled eight full loads to-day!" he exclaimed. "It's appetizing work shovelling coal—isn't it, Tuttle?" This to the head butler, who followed at his heels, and kept sober and worked faithfully as long as Billy had him in sight.

"Dear me!" sighed Mrs. Lumley-Gotham. "When I think of the winter, I don't know how we are going to get through it! Fancy the bedrooms! We'll be frozen to the bones!"

"I am going to sleep by the kitchen stove!" said Reggie.

"Let me catch you!" snorted the old lady.

The discussion was interrupted by the arrival of the Bishop with his arms full of wood. "There!" he exclaimed to the Mistress of the Kitchen. "I hope that'll suit you!"

"That's fine," said Billy, whose task it was to praise and encourage everyone. "Where are you working now?"

"I've begun on the seats at the Pennsylvania depot."

"That ought to last you quite a while!" Then, espying de Puyster in the neighbourhood of the telephones, Billy inquired, "What's the news to-day?"

The reporter put his fingers to his lips, and whispered, "Rare news! A dreadful scandal in an old and highly respected family!"

Billy didn't ask what the scandal was, for at this moment Helen entered, and it was painfully apparent that everybody knew. He took the girl's hand in his—quite shamelessly, before the whole community. "Well, my love," he asked, "how are things going?"

"We had a lesson in sweeping to-day," said Helen. "We're learning wonderfully!"

There was a pause; then Billy turned to the others. "Well, friends, what have you got to say to us? The month is up to-day." He waited, but no one spoke. "We want an answer," he insisted.

"Billy," pleaded Mrs. Lumley-Gotham, "what can you expect us to say?"

"Oh!" he exclaimed. "You haven't changed?"

"I'm almost distracted with worry over it," the old lady answered. "Helen, I don't see how——"

"For heaven's sake," broke in Reggie, "have we got to settle this before supper?"

"Reggie, shut up!" said Eloise.

"Helen," continued Mrs. Lumley-Gotham, "I don't see how you can put such a proposition before your mother. As carefully as I brought you up——"

"Wait, mother, please," said Helen, patiently. "Let us find out what the others have to say."

Billy had turned to the Bishop. "You haven't changed your mind?"

"Billy, it is not a question of human minds, which can be changed. It is a question of God's law."

"I see," said Billy.

"You are considering your own selfish

happiness. But I, who am charged with responsibility for the welfare of all society——"

"But, great heavens, man, can't you see that if Helen and I don't marry, there won't be any society to consider?"

"That may be so," replied the Bishop. "I'm not to blame for that, however. Better no society at all than one founded upon mortal sin."

"And such taste, Helen!" broke in Mrs. Lumley-Gotham. "If you were a common plebeian woman, I could understand——"

"For my part," put in the cynical Sarita, "I wish to God we had a few common plebeian women to wash these dishes!"

Billy could not give up trying to appeal to them. "Somehow or other life must be continued. We've got to create a new race on the earth; and how else can it be managed?"

At this moment a new figure appeared in the doorway. Helen's husband, St. Erskine Granville, was slightly drunk—he had never been entirely sober since the great explosion; but he still managed to keep his fastidious appearance, and his face still wore its smile of mocking cynicism.

"Really now," he declared, "it seems that I have been overlooked."

Those who stood nearest moved away, as if thereby expressing the annoyance which his presence caused them. But this only added to his amusement. He took a seat and looked about him. "Of course, as you know, it is up to me to setfle this matter by challenging Billy to a duel; but how can I do it—having no one to act as my second?" There was a pause; then suddenly he began to sniff. "What odour lures my senses? Potatoes boiling? Mrs. Lumley-Gotham, it was the thought of your cooking which drew me from my contemplation of the vanity of human existence. I wonder, is there anyone in the world who peels potatoes like Sarita Knicker-bocker-Smythe? I wonder if, since the days of Abraham Lincoln, there has been a more valiant wood-chopper than my friend, the Lord Bishop of Harlem?"

The Bishop bowed gravely, in acknowledgment of the compliment. The other added, "I trust Your Grace stands fast for the sanctity of the home?"

The Bishop did not answer. "You will not forget, Your Grace, the many favours which the church received during my administration as Secretary of State. The repeal of the odious church property tax; the extension of free transportation to Sunday school teachers and choir-boys——"

Said the Bishop, with his most earnest manner, "If I support you in this present painful controversy, it is not because of such considerations. The approval of the church is not to be purchased, her judgment is not swayed by the winds of politics."

"Ah, to be sure!" exclaimed Granville. "So much the better! And you, Mrs. Lumley-Gotham—surely worldly misfortune has not caused you to forget the traditions of your noble ancestry! Surely the name of Viviana Athelstan de Smithkins Lumley-Gotham is not to be dragged in the mire of domestic scandal!"

"It is *not!*" exclaimed Mrs. Lumley-Gotham, promptly.

"Ah!" laughed the other. "With two such supports I stand like the colossus! The church and good society on my side! And one more power—the press! What has Mr. de Puyster to say?"

"In such a matter," said de Puyster, "a

journalist must bow to the decision of society's leader." In accordance with his words, de Puyster bowed.

Granville continued, with his most urbane smile, and looking out of the corner of his eyes at Billy. " It is difficult to see how revolution can make bold to raise its horrid front in the face of such authority. But let us at least hear what the rebels say."

Billy started somewhat vehemently : " What the rebels say——"

But Helen stopped him with a cajoling smile. " Billy, the odour of boiled potatoes is unfavourable to the activities of the higher thought centres. I suggest that we all go in to supper, and continue the debate later on."

Here, for the first time, Lumley-Gotham himself made his voice heard. " That's the way to talk ! " And the head butler and Reggie joined the applause.

In the harmony which resulted, there was one discord—the voice of Eloise, in its iciest tones. " I want to make this one statement. I have no objection to setting the table for company, but I do object to washing dishes for them. Do you understand what I mean, Mr. Granville ? "

"I understand perfectly, Eloise," laughed the other, with his most charming society manner. "Hereafter I will carry my soiled dishes away with me whenever I come."

"Come on, mother," said Helen, "you have been working so hard, you must eat." She pushed them into the other room. "Come, de Puyster, come, Bishop—there is nothing heretical in the supper menu, at least."

Said Eloise: "What I can't understand is how my sister can want to cast a shadow upon my name——"

"Eloise," laughed Helen, "will you take in the potatoes?"

"And knowing," persisted the other, "that the man has lost his social position and become an adventurer!" Thus she followed Helen into the room where the supper table was set.

Granville stood watching them, and turned to Sarita with the laughing remark, "Who could believe that so small a world could prove so entertaining!"

"You have always found the world entertaining," she answered him, coldly.

"My dear Sarita," he responded, "have

you not heard the saying that life is a comedy to those who think and a tragedy to those who feel?"

"What is it," she responded, "to those who get drunk?"

"My dear lady, I did my thinking first!" he laughed.

"I see," she said. "You could think of nothing better to do than to drink; and now you see a group of people trying to make the best of a cruel situation, and all you can do is to bedevil them—to go about sticking pins into them, and enjoying their distress!"

"My dear Sarita! How little you comprehend my philosophic mind!"

"What is it? You don't love Helen, I know. Is it that you hate her—and can't let her be happy? Or is it Billy that you hate?"

"It may be a little of both, Sarita. I would not claim to be beyond human weakness. But mainly it is a religious motive that impels me."

Said the woman, sarcastically: "Of course, I am a fool to you—everybody is. But if it would not be too tedious to explain yourself——"

" Not at all, Sarita. We are all fools before we become philosophers. But I got over my folly when I was young. I looked at life from every aspect, and I saw that it was a trap of nature. Every intellectual man discovers that —there is no conceivable end to it, no meaning, no excuse. But what the thinker discovers, he never dares to practice, seldom even to teach. There is that dreadful thing we call morality! There is life, blind, insistent— screaming like a starving infant. ' Let me exist! Let me go on! ' And there is the philosopher who dares to say : ' Strangle it, stifle it, put an end to it ! ' "

" You are that philosopher? " asked Sarita.

" There comes a cataclysm, Sarita ; and so, what I, the philosopher, have always known, suddenly becomes clear even to fools. So at last I am moved to have the courage of my immorality ! "

" Granville," said Sarita, " sometimes I think you are a fiend ! "

" No more babies ! " he laughed. " No more life—at least not if I can help it ! "

" There are Eloise and Reggie ! Watch out for them ! "

" There is little hope for posterity in that

puny pair. And as for you, Sarita, and your longing for me——"

"What?" cried Sarita, aghast.

"As for you, I say——"

She stared at him in fury. "How dare you!"

"My dear," he said, "you must believe me—I am truly sorry to disappoint you. But having this deep philosophic conviction——"

"Granville, you are insolent!"

He was gazing at her intently. "The life-force says, 'If only he would! If only I could blind him, drug him, make him drunk with sensation! If only that brain would go to sleep——"

"Stop!" she cried.

He laughed; but then while he watched her, there came the sound of loud voices from the other room. He listened, and began to laugh. "The argument has begun again!"

Reggie came, following Eloise into the kitchen. "I don't care! I've a right to express my opinion!"

"She's my sister! I'm the one it concerns —not you!"

"Even so," insisted Reggie, "it seems to me——"

" Oh, shut up ! " exclaimed the girl.   " I'm tired of hearing you ! "

" I don't want to argue.   But I just say——"

" Won't you stop?   I don't care what you say——"

" But if she really loves him——"

" Will you get the apple-sauce and take it in? "

" Helen is a grown woman——"

" Give me that bowl for the potatoes ! "

" And we've no right, now that we're all alone——"

" Get out of my way ! " cried Eloise.   She was emptying the steaming potatoes into a huge bowl.   " Decency is decency, I say, whether you're alone or in a crowd ! "

" You deny that she has a right to love? "

" Why doesn't she learn to love her husband? " cried Eloise.   " Other women have to learn, whether they want to or not."

" She never should have married that husband," he answered.   " They made her do it."

Eloise shifted the bowl of potatoes to her other arm, and shook her fist at him furiously. " We didn't ! "

"Everybody knows that she hated him———"

"You ought to be ashamed of yourself. I tell you———" At which moment the huge bowl of potatoes slid from under Eloise's arm and went crashing to the floor. The potatoes they had been labouring all afternoon to prepare!

"Our supper!" wailed Reggie.

Several others came rushing from the dining-room, with a chorus of agonized exclamations. "You wretch!" shrieked the mother.

"I couldn't help it," sobbed the girl. "He's worried the life out of me! This everlasting arguing, arguing! I declare I'll go mad if it doesn't stop!"

"All our supper!" moaned the Bishop. He stooped and picked up one of the hot potatoes and began furtively nibbling it, while Lumley-Gotham possessed himself of a handful and slunk off to one side to eat them.

"I declare," exclaimed his wife, "if this argument doesn't end I shall lie down and die!"

"I say let's end it right now!" cried Billy, impatiently. "Let's end it before supper! I've been thinking it over, and I see a way that will satisfy you, I think—a decent, proper and conventional way."

" What way? " asked Mrs. Lumley-Gotham.

" Simply this—Helen must get a divorce from Granville."

There was an exclamation in chorus. " A divorce! "

" And then," added Billy, " the Bishop can marry us."

" What? " cried the Bishop. " I marry a divorced woman? "

" Now surely, Bishop——" began Helen.

But he would not let her say a word. " Never! Never! You might just as well not talk on that subject."

" Well," said Billy, " if that's the case, we'll have a civil marriage."

" But how? " cried several at once.

Granville interposed. " If I might make a suggestion, you'd better decide about the divorce first. How can you get that? "

Said Mrs. Lumley-Gotham, with great distress of spirit, " There is only one ground for divorce in New York state."

" And all the witnesses are dead," added Granville.

"Well," suggested Billy, "we can go to another state."

"What state?" asked the other.

"New Jersey."

"But then, you have to have a year's residence!"

"They can go to Reno!" exclaimed Sarita.

"But when they get there they won't find any judge!"

"We'll manage it another way," said Billy. "We'll change the law!"

"Change the law!" exclaimed Granville.

"Surely. Why not?"

"Change the divorce laws of New York state?" cried Mrs. Lumley-Gotham. "They haven't been changed in three hundred years."

"All the more reason for changing them now."

"But how can you do it?"

"Have the legislature pass a bill."

"There is no legislature!"

"Well, let's elect one."

"Elect a legislature!" cried the Bishop, in consternation.

"Haven't we just as good a right to elect a legislature as anybody that ever lived?

Aren't we free American citizens, with the right to make our laws? "

They all stood staring, helpless before this proposition. " Billy ! " gasped Mrs. Lumley-Gotham, " you can't mean such a thing ! "

" But I *do* mean it," he responded. " We'll elect a legislature and a governor; a judge, too, while we are about it. We'll pass a law that will allow Helen a divorce——"

" On what ground? " inquired Granville.

" Let me see," reflected Billy. " Desertion."

" But it was she deserted me ! "

" Well, then, how about drunkenness? " And watching the other's face, the young man burst into laughter.

A silence followed. At last Helen spoke. " Yes," she said, " that solves the difficulty ! It will be quite legal and proper——"

" Even fashionable, I should say," added Sarita.

Helen turned to her mother. " What do you think? "

" Why, I don't know. We never had a divorce in our family. But—I suppose——"

She was interrupted by a cry from Eloise. " Mother ! You can't mean to consent? "

" You object? " demanded Billy.

" I think it's perfectly outrageous! If my sister did such a thing, what chance of marriage would I have? "

The young aeronaut turned to the Bishop. " How about you? "

" Sir," was the stately reply, " the attitude of my church on the question of divorce is not determined by legislatures."

" I am to understand that you oppose the plan? "

" I oppose it," said the Bishop, " with all the authority I possess. I oppose it in the name of common decency, of American traditions and institutions, of the church and the faith I represent! I denounce your proposed measure as unconstitutional, null and void; as anarchistic, polygamous, and incendiary; as subversive of morality and the social order, a menace to the sanctity of the home, to the very existence of society. Adverse as I have been to dragging the church into political controversy, I warn you that I shall consider it my solemn duty to rise in that legislature and make a speech against the bill! I warn you in the name of religion——"

" Just wait, Bishop," interposed Helen,

smiling. "The legislature isn't in session yet."

Granville was laughing. "It looks as if you couldn't carry the election, Billy."

"Let's see where we stand," suggested Sarita.

"Let's have a straw ballot!" put in Reggie.

Said the Bishop: "I protest against this farcical trifling with sacred things!"

"Just wait," said Billy, leading Helen to one side. Then to the company, "Those who will vote for the new law will please join us—those who oppose it will stand over there."

Sarita came over promptly. "I am with you."

Eloise was equally prompt in moving to the other side. The Bishop joined her. "I protest," said he. "And so does the church!"

"We'll count that as one vote, if you don't mind," replied Billy.

"And you, mother?" inquired Helen.

The great lady stood hesitating. "I want the thing done decently. I think—I think —I'll have to vote——"

There came an exclamation from Granville. " You *vote?* "

She looked at him. " I vote in favour of the law," she said.

" Mrs. Lumley-Gotham a suffragette ! " cried the other.

Instantly the voice of de Puyster was raised. " What's that? Let me get that ! " He took out his notebook and began to scribble with extraordinary rapidity.

Meantime Billy turned to the poet. " How about you, Reggie? "

Reggie was looking serious. " The way it seems to me——" he began.

" Reggie," broke in Eloise, " you shut up ! "

He stood hesitating. Said the girl: " Reggie, if you don't come here, I'll never marry you, not if you're the last man on earth ! "

Said Sarita : " I call that corrupting the electorate ! "

Reggie moved over to the side of Eloise, and Billy turned to de Puyster. " How about you? "

" De Puyster," said Mrs. Lumley-Gotham, " you told me you accepted my authority in social matters."

" Yes, Mrs. Lumley-Gotham."

" Then come here," she commanded; and he moved to her side.

" That evens the corruption," said Granville.

" Now, Tuttle? " inquired Helen.

" What do you say, Tuttle? " inquired Mrs. Lumley-Gotham.

" Tuttle," interposed the Bishop, " you belong to the church, do you not? "

" Yes, sir."

" Tuttle," broke in Granville, " did you ever hear of divorce for drunkenness? "

" No, sir," said the head butler.

" Just think," persisted the other—" think of all the Christian homes you'd break up by such a law! "

" Tuttle," commanded the Bishop, " come here! "

" Tuttle," cried Mrs. Lumley-Gotham, " you dare to oppose your mistress? "

But Tuttle had moved to the side of the Bishop. Granville joined him, and then the two lines stood surveying each other. There was a tie—five on each side—and it was up to Lumley-Gotham to cast the deciding vote.

In one voice they called him: "Mr. Lumley-Gotham!"

He had just finished his potatoes, having paid no attention to the controversy. Now he started and stared at them, crying, "No, no!"

"But you must!" insisted his wife.

"I will have nothing to do with it!"

"Come, father!" pleaded Helen. "Be sensible."

"Mr. Lumley-Gotham," interrupted Granville, "don't you remember how that last man who threw a bomb at you said it was because of the part you took in politics?"

Whereat Lumley-Gotham himself declared, more vehemently than before, "I'll have nothing to do with it!"

"But, father!" cried Helen.

"I insist!" exclaimed Mrs. Lumley-Gotham, and dragged him to her side. Eloise seized him by the arm and sought to drag him to hers. In the end the old man tore himself loose, and fled into the other room, shouting, "No! No! No!"

"It looks as if we had reached a deadlock," laughed Granville.

"Is there nobody on the other side who will change his vote?" asked Billy.

" Never ! " exclaimed the Bishop.

" Never ! " echoed Eloise. She gave Reggie a vicious pinch, and then he, too, repeated the word. The Bishop looked sternly at Tuttle, who followed suit; and Granville ended the chorus.

" There followed a long pause. " Very well," said Billy, at last, " I see the game is up. There remains to us only the last right of oppressed peoples—the right of revolution ! "

" What do you mean by that ? " demanded Granville.

" Fortunately we don't have to trouble you —your government or your laws—as revolutionists in the past have had to do. We will leave this city to the defenders of law and order; and Helen and I will go away—alone, or with those who care to follow us. We shall found a new colony, where free institutions will prevail ! "

" Billy Kingdon ! " cried Mrs. Lumley-Gotham.

" There is nothing else to be done," he replied. " There is nothing more to be said about it, that I can see. You will go with me, Helen ? "

" I will go," she answered.

" And you, Sarita? "

Sarita answered promptly, " You bet! "

" And you, Mrs. Lumley-Gotham? "

" What an interesting situation! " chuckled Granville. " Mrs. Lumley-Gotham residing in a free-love colony! "

The old lady turned away and hid her face in her hands. Never had she expected to hear such awful words, even in jest. " I cannot go! " she exclaimed.

So Billy turned to de Puyster. " You? " he asked.

" I? " cried the reporter. " If Mrs. Lumley-Gotham disapproves, how could you expect me to go? "

" Very well, then," said Billy. " We three——"

Suddenly Lumley-Gotham himself appeared in the doorway. " You're not going away, Billy? " he cried, in agitation.

" I am," was the reply.

" And Helen? "

" Yes, Helen."

" Then I will go, too! "

" Not much you will! " laughed Billy.

" Wh-w-what? Why not? " stammered the old man.

" Because you wouldn't vote for us."

He answered, " But I *will* vote for you ! "

" What? " cried the opposition, furiously.

" Then we won't need to go ! " shouted Billy.

Eloise sprang at the old man. " Father ! What do you mean? How dare you? "

At which Lumley-Gotham stammered, " No, no, no—I won't——" and backed out of the room in haste.

" Very well," said Billy ; and being young and enthusiastic, he addressed the company in a sudden burst of eloquence. " Stay in this world of darkness and misery that you create and maintain ! Stay and tangle yourself in the net you weave out of your own ignorance and superstition. As for us, we go to a new world, where the rights of the mind are recognized—a world whose laws are made for men ! And let me tell you what will be its marriage law—the law for which I personally will live, and if need be die—that there can be no blacker crime against life than the begetting of a child without love ! "

All were silent. When Billy spoke again, it was to his own party. " Come—friends— we have no belongings to pack, and we will

waste no tears of parting. Let us find ourselves an automobile and go our way. Come,
Sarita! Come Helen—my wife!"

Billy, Helen and Sarita Knickerbocker-
Smythe took an automobile and drove up the
Hudson River to the magnificent country
estate of the Lumley-Gothams in the
Pocantico hills; that evening they were
wandering about in the halls of a great castle,
stored with the art treasures of the last five
thousand years of human history. The
splendour of the structure was overwhelming,
but it was long before the adventurers were
able to overcome the sense of desolation which
weighed upon them.

They had a solemn talk, the evening of their
arrival. They were founding a new civilization, and had a sense of their grave responsi-
bilities. Thousands of years of human
history lay behind them—and all of it a chaos
of blood and tears and suffering! Poets had
sung, prophets had preached, scientists had
studied—and the best they had been able to
produce was a world in which millions of
abject and degraded people toiled without
cease, in order that a few hundred idle

parasites might squander the surplus of their labour.

"You know," said Billy, " how I struggled to change all this. You know our attempts at revolution, and how they were crushed. But now this wickedness has been swept away, and we have a new start; let us make up our minds that we will start right. It won't be long, I feel sure, before some of the others will have enough of their superstitions, and want to join our community. There will be children, and life will start again; let us make up our minds now, in advance, that we will have no more slavery, no more feudalism, no more capitalism! Let us lay, now at the beginning, the foundations of the Co-operative Commonwealth, and insist that everyone who comes to join us shall come on these terms."

So spoke Billy, and it was agreed that day; they drew up a paper and signed it, and thus began the foundation for the new civilization. The three owned the estate in common, and the means of production in common. They worked, each according to his ability, and took of the product each according to his needs. Meantime, they waited to see what would happen to those who were left behind, amid the superstitions and prejudices of the ancient regime.

Things had begun to happen quickly at the Consolidated Hotel. Under the sway of Billy Kingdon, Tuttle, the head butler, had become a sober and diligent shoveller of coal; but the instant Billy's authority was withdrawn, he celebrated his emancipation by going on a spree, turning up at the hotel after all its respectable guests had retired.

He had not had any supper, and was hungry. There was nothing at hand, so he proceeded to rout out the others, ordering them to prepare him a meal. When Reginald Simpkins protested, he was knocked down with a blow; and that was the beginning of trouble for the unfortunate community. All his life Tuttle had been a menial, cringing and obeying the orders of others. Now he was the strongest man in the crowd, and everybody else was afraid of him. From the time he made this discovery he became a brutal tyrant, and the rest were helpless.

In the morning he was surly because he had drunk too much. He wanted coffee, and wanted it quickly. He issued his orders to de Puyster, who was occupied in trying to telephone to the newspapers an account of last night's disturbance. When de Puyster did not obey, Tuttle gave him a kick which sent him half-way across the room; and when Mrs. Lumley-Gotham protested, Tuttle swore at her, and ordered her to have his coffee ready in the future when he awakened. He paced up and down the room, growling and muttering to himself, everybody shrinking into corners to keep out of his way.

They served his coffee, and prepared his breakfast, and he sat at the table alone, devouring his food with as much enjoyment as his headache permitted. It had been one of Billy Kingdon's rules that no liquor should be permitted in the establishment; but Tuttle now called for a supply of whisky and soda, and Reggie, who had learned the lesson of the night before, fled to obey. Unfortunately, however, he stopped outside the room to taste the liquor, and Tuttle, seeing him, forced him to jump for his life from a second-storey window.

All this made a terrifying state of affairs. When Tuttle had drunk himself to sleep—which happened in the course of the afternoon —the company held an anxious consultation.

" The man is a fiend ! " declared Reggie.
" He'll murder us all ! If you could only see
the bruises on my back ! "

" It's outrageous ! " exclaimed the Bishop.
" He actually told me to go to hell ! "

Something must be done. But it was like
the old fable of the mice and the cat—there
was no one to do it ! Billy was gone, and the
terrible truth came to them that he had left
no address !

" We ought to have kept him with us ! "
moaned Reggie. " We were fools to oppose
him ! "

" Reggie," cried Eloise, " you shut up ! "

But Reggie for once was not to be sat upon.
" You wait," he said, " until Tuttle's given
you a beating ! "

" Given me a beating ! " The girl's eyes
flashed. " I should like to see him ! "

" He'll do it," said Reggie, " you see !
Just you let the potatoes burn ! "

" I would kill him, if he dared ! " she
exclaimed. But all the same it was to be
noted that Eloise was silent and thoughtful
during the rest of the discussion.

They dared not talk very long—for Tuttle
had developed an astounding fastidiousness as

to his meals! They set to work at their appointed tasks, but no longer with the enthusiasm which had been inspired by the example of Billy and Helen. Reggie moaned and lamented while he carried the coal, and tears ran down the cheeks of His Grace, the Lord Bishop of Harlem, while he chopped the wood. And then, when the labour was done, there sat a red-faced, insolent brute, in his shirt-sleeves at the table, eating with his knife, and growling every time some article of food was out of his reach.

It was really terrible! Day after day the head butler grew worse, until he came to assume to the imagination of the unhappy people the aspect of a ferocious demon. He drove them about with curses, and blows from a heavy fist. Night after night, when he had fallen into his drunken sleep, they held consultations, in which they planned ways to bind and restrain, or even to kill the monster. But there remained the insuperable difficulty —the binding or killing had to be done with their own hands, and there was no one with the courage to attempt it.

Finally they came to a decision : they must flee! There was a whole city about them—

other hotels where they might live, other stores where they could find food. Let Tuttle have the Consolidated Hotel and everything in it, and they would begin life all over again.

So, in the middle of the night, the party set out: Lumley-Gotham himself, his wife and daughter, the Bishop, the poet laureate and the society reporter. Granville they left behind, because they dared not trust him. He was still leading his solitary life, drinking more or less steadily; and when he came to visit them, it was only to laugh at their troubles. He was the one person who was still able to inspire Tuttle with awe, and who had no fear of the monster's wrath.

They betook themselves to an hotel farther down town—one of the palatial structures located on the East river parkway—and here for a couple of weeks they lived a peaceful existence, so far as their tyrant was concerned. They kept indoors and lighted no fires, and so Tuttle, riding about the city in an automobile, got no clue to their whereabouts.

But such a miserable existence it was! They had nothing to eat but cold canned food —and the kind of food which had been canned in a capitalist civilization! They did not know what the trouble was, but they were beginning to fail in health, and their irritability increased in consequence. There was incessant quarrelling as to the work, and it was not long before Reggie and the Bishop decided to withdraw and set up an establishment of their own. What was the use of women, anyway—when no cooking could be done?

But this selfish move proved the undoing of the two men. For it was not long before they became reckless, and started a fire; and while they were seated at a feast of fried potatoes and bacon, they were horrified to hear the sound of an automobile. They rushed to a window, and there was the demon Tuttle, gazing up at them! "Come down!" he commanded, and added a string of terrifying threats.

There followed a man-hunt, such as might have taken place in primeval forests, when the cave-men preyed upon one another. Tuttle came up one flight of stairs, and Reggie and the Lord Bishop fled down another. But he spied them as they crossed the street; and up to the top of another building he chased them, panting and exhausted. On the roof of the building they separated, and it was the unhappy poet who had the misfortune to be followed.

There came next a scene of horror which we will not inflict upon the reader. Suffice to say that Reggie was caught, and received a beating which caused him to writhe upon the ground in front of his master, pleading for mercy, and promising that he would do anything, that he would obey any orders, that he would never, never make an attempt to escape again. So Tuttle dragged him in, and carried him off to his lair in the Consolidated Hotel.

The master procured a good-sized club, wherewith to impress his victim, and thereafter Reggie lived as Tuttle's cowering and submissive slave. He fetched and carried for him; he prepared his food for him, and served it too, not shrinking from the most menial offices. His spirit was thoroughly broken, and while he dreamed of escape and even of murder, he did nothing.

This state of affairs continued for about a month. But there were limits to the ability of one slave, and in the end Tuttle became ambitious. Why should he not have more than one to wait on him? Also, why should he not, according to the custom of slave-masters throughout all history, have a female slave? As soon as this idea came to him, it haunted and inflamed his drunken mind, until finally he seized his man-Friday, and tortured him until he revealed the hiding-place of the women. After which Tuttle tied up the poet with a rope and set out in his automobile, armed with the club.

He found the place without difficulty, and kept watch until Eloise was alone. Then he sprang out and seized her by the arm, twisting it behind her back after a fashion known to slave-drivers. By this means he compelled her to be silent, and carried her off without anyone else in the party knowing what had happened. When he reached the hotel again, he flung her into the room, and ordered her to assist Reggie in preparing his supper. All of which, you perceive, was according to the customs of the institution of slavery from the earliest times.

But Tuttle had overlooked two circumstances: one, the difficulty of keeping slaves in an age of automobiles; and the other the fact that Reginald Simpkins was in love with Eloise. Their quarrels, violent as they might have seemed to the outsider, were really but a

kind of practice for matrimony; and now,
when Reggie saw his beloved about to become
the victim of a half-drunken servant, he
became desperate. He managed to wriggle
himself free from his bonds, and when Tuttle
stepped out of the room for a moment, he
and the girl fled by another door, reached the
street, and sprang into the automobile.
They were around the corner before Tuttle
discovered the trick, and were out of sight
before he could get another car to follow.

And having once got out of sight, you may
be sure they took pains not to be captured
again. No more hiding in other hotels! No
more city life, but the open country—the
back-to-nature movement for them!

It was a most romantic elopement. For
years the unhappy poet had pined, scarcely
venturing to hint his passion for so
tremendous a personage as the youngest
daughter of the line of Lumley-Gotham.
But now he had saved her life in approved
romantic fashion, so at last he dared to press
his suit. How a daughter of so ancient a
house could consent to dispense with a grand
state wedding, and indeed with any wedding
at all, is a matter upon which we decorously

draw the curtain. Suffice it to say that Reginald and Eloise fled across one of the great bridges which spanned the Hudson River, and spent their unsanctified honeymoon in a suburban village, many miles distant from New York.

Needless to say, the kidnapping of Reggie and Eloise struck terror into the hearts of those who were left behind. They had no means of knowing how the two had made their escape from their cruel master. All they knew was that Tuttle was still roaming about the city, liable to swoop down and carry off another slave at any time. As soon as they had recovered their first shock, they discussed means of protecting themselves against fresh inroads.

Obviously, the first thing was to move to another part of the city, and redouble their precautions to keep hidden. Also they must arm themselves, and in future must resist by force. Mrs. Lumley-Gotham, the one efficient person left with the party, declared that they must establish a system of sentries, so that it would never again be possible for Tuttle to steal into their fortress.

After much discussion, it was agreed that Mrs. Lumley-Gotham should be appointed the head of a defence committee, and that Lumley-Gotham, the Lord Bishop and de Puyster should take their orders from her. They would take turns mounting guard, in watches of four hours. But, alas, it was tiresome business crouching in a doorway, peering up and down the street and listening for the sound of an automobile. It did not take very many turns to break down their determination, and to lead them to forget their peril.

The trouble began when the Lord Bishop was found asleep at his post. It became greater when Lumley-Gotham himself declared that he was too ill—he could not sit up, and he would not attempt to take his turn. That infernal diet of canned food was killing him! They must learn to build a smokeless fire, so that he could boil potatoes and rice.

Which brought their affairs to a crisis. For Mrs. Lumley-Gotham was determined that they must protect themselves; she would *not* have fires, and she *would* have the watch kept. " You have got to mount guard," she declared.

" But I won't ! " he answered.

" Then I'll make you ! "

" What will you do? "

" You take your place at that door, and if I catch you falling off to sleep again, you'll feel a frying-pan over the top of your head."

Now, this was a terrible state of affairs. They had long arguments back and forth, in the course of which the duty of guard mounting was sadly neglected. De Puyster took Mrs. Lumley-Gotham's side. He had been beaten by Tuttle many times, and did not want to be beaten again. He had done his turn; why should the others be allowed to beg off? The Bishop also agreed, provided that somebody would keep him awake; he did not see how he could manage it by himself. The richest man in the world, being left without a supporter, declared, " I'll go off and live by myself."

" You shall *not* go off! " vowed his wife.

" You'll keep me here by force? "

" I'll do just that! You shall stay here and help us fight Tuttle."

" But that's Slavery! " cried Lumley-Gotham. "That's as bad as what Tuttle's done! "

" I don't care what you call it," answered his wife. " I only say you stay ! "

The old man decided to obey; but he would not stop complaining, and all day long and part of the night they argued the question back and forth. Was it Slavery, as he declared—was it brutal, unmitigated, inexcusable Slavery? Had they gone back ten thousand years in the world's history? Mrs. Lumley-Gotham spurned the charge indignantly, declaring that it was not Slavery, but a bulwark against it, an advance to the next highest stage of civilization—to Feudalism! She was the noble lady, mistress of a castle, guardian and protectress of a community; the rest of them were her knights, her clergy—her serfs, if they would have it so. Anyhow, there was no escaping her sway. Just as in the days of Feudalism, the existence of the whole community depended upon obedience. They must all take oath of fealty, and defend their lady to the death—otherwise they would fall prey to the robber-chieftain who prowled about in the forest near their castle.

Lumley-Gotham's protests had continued for about a week, when one day, during his

turn on guard, he espied Granville passing
down the street. The thought flashed over
him that here was a chance of deliverance.
Granville was the one person who was strong
enough to oppose his terrible wife! Without
waiting to consult the rest, he signalled to his
former Secretary of State, who first started in
surprise, and then came over and joined him
in the doorway, and listened to his complaints.

Granville's sardonic spirit was delighted
with the problem the old man put before him.
Was it Slavery, or was it Feudalism? The
ex-secretary discussed the question with much
gravity, bringing out stores of legal learning,
and quoting historical authorities.

They were still in the midst of the
discussion when Mrs. Lumley-Gotham
appeared. She was distressed because their
whereabouts had been revealed; but she
decided to enlist Granville on their side. He
was the one man who was able to hold Tuttle
in check. Could not he be persuaded to join
forces with them and protect them?

Granville listened for a while, and then,
with the utmost seriousness, took up the
discussion from Lumley-Gotham's point of
view. An enlightened and cultured man, the

former Secretary of State of the United States of the Western Hemisphere, he could not lend his sanction to the system of Slavery, which had incurred the disapprobation of the world's most enlightened thinkers. But Feudalism—that was something quite different! To be a feudal lord, with bishops and knights and loyal retainers, with stately dames to grace one's festal board and with bold archers to defend one's castle against robbers and marauders—that indeed would thrill the soul of a man of culture and poetic sensibility! If they would see fit to give him the title of Baron Granville; if they would revive the ancient ceremonies, and swear upon their swords to follow him to the death; if they would make him their liege lord, and give him the power of life and death over them —then he might consent to dwell with them, and protect them against the furious Attila Tuttle! And so at last it was agreed, and civilization passed by formal decree into a new era.

Now, as the reader may already know, Feudalism, representing a higher stage of civilization, never failed to supplant the more primitive stage whenever the two came into conflict. The same day that the compact was concluded, Granville took his trembling retainers in an automobile to the Consolidated Hotel, where originally they had made their home. He sought out Tuttle, and informed him that hereafter Baron Granville and his feudal community were the masters of the place; that they proposed to stand together, and fight to the death, and that Tuttle, the slave-driver, would molest them at his peril.

And Tuttle, the slave-driver, first blustered, and then, meeting the gaze of Baron Granville's eyes, and noting his mocking smile, gave way. He would take himself off, and trouble them no more.

Said Granville, "If you get lonely, you will be welcome at any time to join us; all you have to do is swear allegiance to me, and recognize my authority."

"You go to hell!" was Tuttle's answer; and he got into his automobile and rode away, with several cases of the finest brand of champagne from the hotel cellars.

The inauguration of the new civilization was celebrated with a banquet of many kinds of delicious freshly-cooked foods. So reassured were they by the protection of their new lord, that they gave up their watch, and for two or three weeks lived an existence which, in comparison with what had gone before, might almost have been called happy.

History records that the feudal stage of society lasted five or six hundred years, and that the forces which brought it to an end were the invention of gunpowder and printing. It may, perhaps, be taxing the reader's credulity to state that in this new community it lasted only five or six weeks. But the fact was that certain economic forces were at work among the retainers of Baron Granville, which made certain the rapid modification of his regime.

You see, the guests of the Consolidated Hotel were not thriving upon their fare of canned stuff. They knew nothing about the chemistry of what they were eating, but they knew that they had a wild and constantly increasing craving for fresh foods—for anything which had not come out of a can. Before the cataclysm which had destroyed the rest of the world, Lumley-Gotham himself had been living upon a special diet, contrived for him by the most learned scientists of that time. There had been a wonderful food tablet which he had swallowed every two hours, upon which he thrived marvellously. His physicians had warned him that if he ate other foods he would not live very long; so now he was haunted by the image of immediate dissolution.

He had none of the precious tablets in his possession, and did not know where to find any. He did not know the formula by which they were made—in fact, he knew nothing about them except that they were brought to him every two hours upon a golden tray.

But Tuttle, who had to do with the serving of them, and had known where they were made, took a trip to the Pleasure Palace, and climbed about eighty flights of stairs and found a small store of the precious objects. He thrived upon them so marvellously that he made further investigations and discovered the laboratory where they were prepared.

The formula was simple, and it was not long before the head butler had learned to work the machinery and make the tablets. And when he had done this his heart leaped with delight. He was the discoverer of a secret which was essential to the existence of the others. He was the new master of the world!

At first, so great was his hatred of Baron Granville and his retainers, he decided to keep the secret, and let the rest of them die in misery. But then the idea flashed over him, why not sell his tablets. Sell them at a high price, and make the others work for him! That would be better than Slavery! That would be Business!

When this idea flashed over the head butler's mind, he fairly shouted with glee, and forthwith sprang into his automobile and journeyed to the Consolidated Hotel. His arrival caused great excitement among the guardians of the castle, for it chanced that the Baron was away at the time. They were in terror of their lives; but Tuttle made haste to reassure them. In the course of his absence he had had time to think things over, and had realized the difference between a slave-driver and a business man. The slave-driver is big and brutal, with a harsh voice and a red face and a strong fist; but the business man is well dressed and polite, and does not depend upon his muscles.

" You have nothing to fear from me," said

Tuttle. "I'm entirely reformed—I'm goin' to obey all the laws."

"You—you really mean that?" stammered Lumley-Gotham, who was on guard at the time, and whose duty it was to kill Tuttle on sight.

"Take it easy," said the head butler. "I've come to bring you help."

The others had come running to the door, and were staring. "Bring us help!" echoed Mrs. Lumley-Gotham.

"Yes," was the reply. "I think we've had enough quarrelling, and I've got a scheme to fix things up."

"What is it?"

But he would not tell them. "Wait till Granville comes back. He's still your boss, ain't he?"

"Our Baron," said de Puyster, gravely.

"All right," said the other. "Whatever he is, I'll talk it out with him first."

Supper was ready, and with some trepidation they invited Tuttle to share it with them; but to their surprise he refused. "I ain't eatin' that sort of food just now," he said. But that was all they could get him to tell. He was a business man, he said, and his affair was with the Government, not with subordinates and inferiors.

Baron Granville returned, and there was a secret conference in one of the remote rooms of the Consolidated Hotel. It was not the first time that important deals between statesmen and business men had been consummated in that establishment; and perhaps we shall be accused of muck-raking if we venture to tell exactly what happened. But a faithful historian will not let himself be swayed from the path of duty by fear of criticism. Posterity demands, and will have, the truth.

Tuttle's proposition was simple. He had the real thing in food, and the rest of them could get along without it. He had torn up the formula—the secret of the all-precious health tablets existed in his mind and nowhere else. There was no way for the rest to get it, save by making terms with him. He would make the tablets, and would sell them to the others for a price.

" What price? " asked Granville, promptly.

" Now you people have got to understand," said Tuttle, " that you've got to have these tablets, or you die. Most of your cans will bust when freezing-time comes, and then where will you be? "

" Tell me your price," said Granville.

" You can go on for a while," continued Tuttle, implacably. " You'll fight me off, but you'll get sicker and sicker, and in the end, to save your lives you'll have to come across."

" It is really a wonderful work that you have done, Mr. Tuttle," said the Baron, tactfully. You may be sure that the word *Mr.* was not overlooked by the head butler, who never before had been thus addressed.

" I know it's a wonderful work," he said, complacently.

" You have conferred a benefit upon humanity, one which will for ever make your name illustrious. That must be a source of gratification to you."

" I'm gratified, all right," said the head butler, his little pig's eyes twinkling.

" And surely you will not be too hard in your requirements—will not wish to withhold from your fellow men the benefit of such vital knowledge. You will be generous——"

Said Tuttle : " Now look-a-here, Mr. Granville——"

"*Baron*," corrected the other.

"Now look-a-here, don't you try to come any such game as that over me! I'm a business man! You see?"

"A business man?" said Granville, taken aback for a moment.

"A business man, and I ain't in business for my health. We ain't goin' to have no philanthropy talk in this deal—and you might just as well save your breath, for it won't do no good."

"Ahem!" said the other, controlling his anger—as one must when dealing with business men. "State your terms, Mr. Tuttle."

The other edged a jot nearer, and turned to see that the door was closed. "Now listen," he said, "there's no reason why you and me should quarrel. We are the only people in this crowd that are fit for anything. Why shouldn't we stand together, and make the rest work for us?"

"I am sure, Mr. Tuttle, I am perfectly willing to consider a proposition. I have no hard feelings towards you."

"All right," said Tuttle, "then let's get down to business. I started to make these people work for me, and they wouldn't do it.

Maybe I was a little harsh about it. I'm willing to admit that—I was drunk at the time, and a man isn't exactly what he ought to be when he's drunk. You understand?"

"Perfectly," said Granville, with a smile.

"Well, they got away from me, and I ain't tried to get them back. I saw it would mean a fight, and maybe I'd get hurt, and what was the use? But now you've got them to obeyin' you, an' everything goin' nice. You've got a government—a sort of——"

"A feudal society," put in the other.

"I don't know anything about feudal society, but I know what business is, and this looks to me like a good thing. Now you go in with me, and we'll sell these here tablets to the rest of 'em, and we'll make 'em pay. See?"

Granville had become more cordial. "An excellent scheme, Mr. Tuttle. But understand, of course, I have to have some of the tablets also."

"Sure!" said Tuttle. "That's what I'm talking about." He drew his chair closer, and began to tap with his finger upon Granville's knee. "This is the way I figure it out. These people have to have a tablet every two hours. That's eight of 'em every day, allowing for eight hours' sleep. I don't see that there's any need of their sleeping that long, but we'll let it go for the present. The point is, we'll give them eight tablets for sixteen hours' work, and that'll be their wages."

" I see," said Granville.

" That'll keep 'em goin', and there's no reason why they shouldn't get along and be contented. They don't need anything but food; they can go out and get their clothes for nothing——"

" They won't have much time to go out," suggested the Baron, " if they have to work sixteen hours a day."

" Well," said Tuttle, " they can wear the clothes what they've got for the present, and we'll consider the rest by and by. The point is, we'll make them the proposition to give them a tablet every time they work two hours—whatever kind of work we tell 'em to do."

" But where do I come in ? " asked Granville.

" You? " said Tuttle. " Why, you'll be the boss——"

" Baron," corrected Granville.

"Well, Baron. Naturally, being a noble-man, you wouldn't be expected to work. My idea is that you and I ought to be able to get along comfortable on the work of the other four, and if you'll manage 'em, and see that they do what they're told—why, that's an important service, and naturally, I'd expect to pay you for it."

"And the pay will be?" inquired Granville.

"Why, you'll get your eight tablets a day for the job of bossing——"

"Governing, we call it," corrected the baron.

"Well, governing. You'll get your eight tablets every day, and you'll be able to live like a gentleman, the same as me."

There was a pause while Granville considered the proposition. The other was watching him anxiously. "It seems to me that's a fair offer," Tuttle argued. "It's really exactly the same as it used to be in the old world. You're the politician, the man that governs—and I'm the business man, the one that owns things. The rest of 'em, they're the ones that do the work. We'll be able to live fairly decent—we can have the place kept clean and comfortable, and somebody to wait on us when we're tired; and if any of 'em make a fuss, or don't do their work right, why all we have to do is to fire 'em, and they don't get their tablets, and then they get sick. From all I can see, it's a proposition you can't get away from."

And Granville rose, with his most genial smile, and stretched out his hand to the head butler. "Mr. Tuttle," he said, "you're a genius! You are what, in the old days, we used to call a man of affairs, a great industrial pioneer. I congratulate you upon the plan which you have evolved, and upon the lucidity with which you have stated it. After listening to you, I feel myself many centuries more advanced in the school of human progress. I become a new kind of nobleman, a modern nobleman. The days of capitalism have begun!"

And so the conference adjourned, and Tuttle, the capitalist, and Baron Granville, the Government, return to discuss matters with the consuming public, which, needless to say, was waiting impatiently to know what had happened.

Tuttle seated himself, and gave a preliminary cough. "Ladies and gentlemen," he began, "I been talking with Mr. Granville——"

"Baron Granville," corrected the other.

"With Baron Granville. I have a most important piece of news. I wanted to be sure I had got things right before I told you about it. The point is, I've been rummaging round, and I've found out the formula for the food tablets which Mr. Lumley-Gotham used to eat."

"Oh!" cried the public, in one breath.

"Give it to me!" cried Lumley-Gotham himself, in great excitement.

"Of course, you understand," continued Tuttle, "it wasn't an easy matter to get a thing like that straight. I've been working like the very deuce, but now I think I've got it all right. I talked it over with the Baron, and he thinks I have, too."

"You can make the tablets?" cried Lumley-Gotham.

"Yep," said Tuttle. "Fact is, I've a pocketful of 'em."

The listeners started to their feet, their faces showing pitiful agitation. "Give us some!"

But Tuttle made no move. "Take it easy, now," he said.

" But you are surely going to give them to us? " cried the Bishop.

Tuttle coughed. " There's a few matters to be talked over," he replied. " You don't suppose I'll give 'em away for nothing, do you? "

Here the Baron stepped in. " If I might make a suggestion, Mr. Tuttle," he said, urbanely, " it would be that you give each of them one or two tablets. That is in accordance with business precedents—a demonstration tablet, so to speak. You want them to know that you've got the real thing."

Tuttle hesitated a moment, and then slowly drew a little box from his pocket and extracted five tablets. He handed one to Granville and one to each of the others.

" You might give me two," suggested Granville, mildly, and the capitalist complied.

The look of eagerness and excitement on the faces of the suffering wretches would have moved any heart not made of stone. They inspected the tablets, then took them in their mouths, and permitted them to dissolve upon their tongues. Oh, what a rare, what a marvellous flavour ! A single look at the face of Lumley-Gotham himself would have told anyone that the head butler had indeed found the formula.

There was general silence while the wonderful morsel melted away. Then came sighs and looks of longing. "I could eat another one," said Lumley-Gotham.

But Tuttle had already restored the box to his pocket. "The order is one every two hours," he declared, decisively. And then, hitching up his chair, "Now let's get down to business. You people want to live on tablets after this, I reckon?"

"Yes, yes," said Lumley-Gotham; and the others nodded.

"Well," said Tuttle, "you understand it has been hard work to make 'em; it will always be hard work. I have talked it over with Baron Granville, and he agrees with me that it is fair. You work for me two hours and you get a tablet."

"But," they cried, "we have to have a tablet every two hours!"

"Exactly," said Tuttle. "You don't have to eat in your sleep, do you?"

"But do we have to work all the time we are awake?" cried the Bishop.

Tuttle shrugged his shoulders. "I don't

care whether you work or not," he said. " I don't care what you do. I'm only telling you on what terms you can have my tablets."

" But," cried Mrs. Lumley-Gotham, " then we can't afford to eat your tablets ! "

The other shrugged his shoulders again. " All right," he said, " you can go without 'em, then."

There was a long silence. It took them a while to realize their plight. " What sort of work do you want us to do? " demanded de Puyster.

" I'll tell you what I want when the time comes," said the other. " I want you to wait on me and Mr. Granville here."

" On Granville? " they cried. " But why should we wait on him? "

" Because," said Tuttle, " he's the Baron. You wouldn't expect a nobleman to work, would you? He's goin' to be—what are you goin' to be, Baron? "

" Ahem ! " coughed Granville, " I will be —say, the Governor-General. I think that's the right title for me. Mr. Tuttle will be the President of the Amalgamated Food Tablets Companies, Limited."

There was again a silence. Nothing more

tragic could have been imagined than the faces of the Baron's unhappy retainers. " Please, please," said the Bishop, finally, " tell us the nature of the work."

" Why," said Tuttle, " you know what work is. You are to wait on us, keep our house decent, bring us drink when we want it—just make yourselves useful."

" You needn't worry," added the Baron— or perhaps we had better say now, the Governor-General—" we'll tell you exactly what we want done."

" But," cried Lumley-Gotham himself, " I can't do such hard work! You know I am an old man."

" We'll let the Bishop here do the hard work," said Tuttle. " He's a good husky chap. Also hard work seems to have agreed with Mrs. Lumley-Gotham."

The Mistress of Society was glaring at him. It was hard to believe that this was the same man who had been her obsequious servant. " How *dare* you! " she exclaimed.

Tuttle went on, without paying attention to this. " You needn't worry; we don't want to make things too hard. You just do what you are told to do, cheerfully and obligingly, and we'll have no trouble, and you'll get your tablets. We don't want to humiliate you— we won't make you put on knee breeches or anything like that. But you might just as well understand at the start, if you want your tablets, you do your work; and any time the work ain't done proper, you'll get fined one tablet. See?"

Mrs. Lumley-Gotham sprang up in fury. "I'll have nothing to do with such arrangement! I'll not eat your tablets!"

"Nor I!" exclaimed the Bishop.

"Nor I!" echoed de Puyster.

Tuttle grinned. "All right," he said, "take your choice about that. You are free citizens, and it's every man's right not to work, if he chooses." He turned to the old man. "How about you?" he inquired.

Lumley-Gotham hesitated. "I—I—you know how it is," he said. "My physician told me—really, you know, it is cruel of you to take advantage of me like this!"

"Will you work or won't you work?" demanded Tuttle.

"I was told," pleaded the old man, "that if I was to live at all——"

"Then you'll work?"

" Yes, I'll work."

" For shame on you, Lumley-Gotham! "
cried his wife.

But the other edged around behind the
burly form of the head butler, who made clear
that he was ready to defend the principles of
freedom of contract and the open shop. So
the others turned and marched sullenly from
the room.

All day long old Lumley-Gotham toddled
about, waiting humbly upon the Governor-
General and the President of the Amalgamated
Food Tablets Companies, Limited. The food
tablet machinery was moved to the Consolidated
Hotel and got into operation, and meantime
the other three members of the rebellious
community cooked themselves canned foods
and suffered intestinal agonies.

" How long do you suppose they'll hold
out? " said Tuttle.

And Granville answered, " I'll fix them in
a day or two."

He got an automobile and rode to the
Executive Buildings, which occupied a square
mile or so of the lower part of the city. In
the police offices he found a copy of a book

which had been suppressed by the government; a lurid volume, full of revolutionary sentiments. Its title was, " The Food Fakers," and it revealed the horrors incidental to the preparation of canned foods for the masses of the population. It showed how the meats were full of anhydrous sodium sulphite, and how the vegetables were preserved with benzoate of soda, and coal tar dyes, having names which took whole paragraphs to print. It made chills run up and down one's spine even to read of these horrors; and the diabolical Granville paid a friendly call upon the three passive resisters, and accidentally left this volume behind him.

The Bishop, an inquisitive person, picked it up. Having the idea that it might contain the secret formula of the food tablets, he read the volume through; and of course he could not keep from talking to the others about it. Thereafter their food was served with a sauce of conversation about anhydrous sodium sulphite and benzoate of soda. Whether it was actually the foods, or whether it was the book, no one can say, but in a week more their resistance was broken, and after many consultations and lamentations, the three of them came to the capitalist and announced their surrender. They would work for him on his own terms; one tablet for two hours' labour, faithfully executed according to orders. The contract was drawn up, and signed in the presence of the Governor-General, and so the capitalist system was at last formally established.

For about a month things went smoothly. Tuttle got drunk a great deal, but he was not allowed to beat or abuse his working people, because there was the Governor-General to preserve order and execute justice. Granville had the traditions of the old regime behind him, and by means of his quiet mockery he held Tuttle up to the standards of the business world. The head butler must remember that he was no longer a slave-driver; he was a gentleman. He must wear decent clothes, and have his shoes shined, no matter how drunk he was. He must be addressed as Mister, and he must show a respect for law and order.

How long things might have continued thus, no one can say. The first break in the system occurred because Tuttle got tired of the labour of preparing the tablets. It took

about a half-day's hard work to prepare a
three days' supply for the whole community,
and Tuttle did not see why he should have to
do such work himself. It was an outrage that
a gentleman should have to stand up over a
steaming kettle mixing food!

"But," exclaimed the Governor-General,
"what else can you do? You can't let them
do the work."

"Damn it!" growled Tuttle. "Why
can't I?"

"You will give away your formula!"

"Well," said the other, "I don't need to
let them use it, do I?"

"How can you prevent it?"

"Easy enough. What are you the Government for?"

"But what can the Government do?"

"Forbid them. Say you'll give them a
licking if they make tablets except for us."

"By jove!" exclaimed the Governor-
General. He sat in thought and suddenly a
look of amusement spread over his countenance. "Why," he exclaimed, "I can issue
you a patent! And then if anybody infringes
it, we can put him in jail!"

"I don't care what you call it," was

Tuttle's response. "What I want you to do is to fix it up so that I don't have to work."

So the Governor-General got the little group together. They were a civilized community, he said, and it was time they had a code of laws. They would first declare the old common law in force, and then they would proceed to consider the question of additional legislation. There had recently been presented a public demand for laws on the subject of patents. It was obviously an important thing to stimulate inventive genius. Nothing could be of greater advantage to the community than for someone to discover new labour-saving machinery, or even how to work the machinery already existing. There should be a law securing to the inventor the fruits of his ingenuity. It was hereby solemnly decreed that anyone who discovered a process or a machine might register his claims with the Governor-General and have the exclusive right to control the use of such a process or machine.

And when this law was fully enacted and written down upon the statute-books, the President of the Amalgamated Food Tablets

Companies, Limited, came forward with a written statement of the formula and the process for the preparation of food tablets. This statement was accepted and filed in the Governor-General's pocket, and the latter made a little speech in which he pointed out the advantages of civilization; it was no longer necessary for Tuttle to hide his knowledge—he could put it on record for the benefit of future generations. Granville appealed to religious sanctions and to patriotic feelings, to the reverence for the great heritage of history and the respect for the sanctities of law; the hearts of his hearers beat fast, and they were proud of being members of a society with such a clever inventor and such an eloquent Governor-General.

But alas! the thermometer of their enthusiasm fell rapidly the next day, when they discovered the real meaning of this patent—that they had to do the work of preparing their own food tablets, and those of Tuttle and Granville as well. Tuttle sat by and fanned himself with a palm-leaf fan (for it was hot weather) while Mrs. Lumley-Gotham stood with a long-handled ladle, stirring the contents of a great cauldron. The

Bishop stripped himself to his under-shirt, and chopped up roomfuls of furniture for firewood. De Puyster fetched and carried and made himself generally useful, while Lumley-Gotham himself toddled here and there, bringing mint-juleps and mineral water for the President of the Amalgamated Food Tablets Companies, Limited.

It has been written that the capitalist system may be likened to an automobile, in that three or four people get the fresh air and the scenery, and the rest of the world gets the dust and the stink. The members of the working class growled and grumbled much, but they didn't see what they could do about it. At the least hint of complaint, Tuttle was ready with his answer : " Go out and live on canned foods and take care of yourself." And when they thought of rebellion, there was the Governor-General with his threats of punishment. They were quite new to the rôle of proletarians, and had to go through the whole painful process.

At first their discontent took the form of schemes of individual advancement. In America everybody has a chance to rise and become president. Let him only use his talents; let him get out and hustle. Go West, young man!

There was de Puyster, for example. He had considerable newspaper training. He had been the leading society reporter of his time—and in the year 2000 the society reporter occupied the place of honour assigned to the base-ball expert in the year 1913. So if only he could persuade the ruling class to take an interest in literature! Would they not, for instance, like to have a daily journal of events? Would they not like to have their laws neatly written out, in the best technical language? De Puyster suggested all these things, but in vain. There was no patron of the arts among the ruling class.

Then came the Bishop. Now that they had got through the period of intense struggle, it was time they began once more to think of their souls. Surely they would not give themselves up exclusively to the sordid material interests of life, forgetting the greater claims of religion! Man does not live by bread alone—nor even by food tablets. There must be some recognition of the significance of the church in modern society.

Thus spoke the voice of His Grace, the Lord

Bishop of Harlem; and he went privately to
see the Governor-General about it. This
matter must not be overlooked, he said; there
was great discontent among the people,
and if their thoughts were not turned away
from worldly things, they might presently
fall prey to demagogic agitators. In the old
days the church had occupied a position of
nearly as great importance as the nobility;
and woe be to that society which degraded
the Vicar of God on Earth into a hewer of
wood and a drawer of water!

The Governor-General listened gravely, and
said he would think it over. There might be
something in it. In these days of modern
science it could hardly be expected that the
church would be restored to the authority it
had held in the middle ages; but there was no
question that it might still fulfil a useful, if
slightly subordinate rôle. " I will talk it over
with Tuttle," said Granville, " and see what
he thinks."

" But why with Tuttle? " demanded His
Grace, who had no great hopes from that
quarter. " Aren't you the Governor-General?
Isn't it for you to say? "

" Just what is your idea? " countered the

Governor-General. " Do you simply want permission to preach to the people? "

" Why," said the other, " I want that, of course, but—I—I have to live——"

" In other words," said the Governor-General, " you want some food tablets free, is that it? "

The Bishop drew himself up with dignity. " You have heard the saying that ' the labourer is worthy of his hire.' "

" Well," said the other, " you understand, the tablets have to come from Tuttle. I haven't got any, except what I eat myself."

" But," protested the Bishop, " if the church is to be endowed——"

Said the Governor-General, " It must be by private individuals. A state-endowed church would be wholly out of the question. You know as well as I do that it is to the capitalist that the bishop has to go for funds."

So to Tuttle the matter came. It was no easy matter to get this hard-boiled captain of industry to subscribe food tablets for the church, but finally, after several conferences, he was persuaded to see it. His Grace, the Lord Bishop of Harlem, was to be a hewer of wood and a drawer of water six days in the

week, but on the Sabbath day he was to
receive his eight food tablets, and in return
was to hold church and preach a sermon to
his congregation.

As to the nature of these sermons Tuttle
was explicit. The Bishop might preach anything he chose about Heaven; he might have
it all his own way so far as the future world
was concerned; but so far as concerned the
affairs of the Consolidated Hotel in the year
2000, his doctrine was to be clear and
unmistakable. He was to preach on the text,
"Render unto Cæsar the things that are
Cæsar's." He was to preach on the text,
"To order myself humbly and lowly towards
all my betters, and to do my duty in that
sphere of life to which it has pleased God to
call me." And yet again on the text,
"Servants obey your masters." And yet
again, "To be respectful to those to whom
God in His infinite wisdom has entrusted the
care of the property interests of the country."

Ambition was stirring also in the soul of
Mrs. Lumley-Gotham. Her duty was to mix
and stir the food tablets, and all the machinery
incidental to their preparation had to be taken
apart and cleaned and put together again

under her direction. She was a capable lady, and she thought about what she was doing. There was part of the machinery which they did not know how to use, and some of the processes took many hours longer than necessary on this account. So came Mrs. Lumley-Gotham's great thought: she would find out about these processes and save time!

Her ambition, you perceive, took the form of legitimate industry. Why should she not be taking out patents? Why should she not become a capitalist, and restore the line of Lumley-Gotham to its former eminence? After working all day, she sat up half the night studying the machinery; and at last— Eureka! She was an inventor!

Also, she was a business woman. She knew that it was necessary to proceed cautiously about such matters. She sat down and wrote out a precise statement of her ideas, in the form of an application for a patent. She secured the signatures of no less than three witnesses to her claims. Then, and then only, she presented the matter to the constituted authorities.

This, of course, meant Granville, who read it over and raised his eyebrows. "Well," he said, "this is very interesting. This is a matter we shall have to look into."

"What looking into does it require?" demanded the applicant. "Issue my patent at once."

"Well," said the Governor-General, "you see—ahem—the matter is complicated. Your patent has to do with processes which have already been patented. It is necessary to consult the records. You see, there is a difficult distinction, and there must be no confusion, no possibility of misunderstanding."

So the applicant went away, and there was a secret conference between Government and Big Business. "What the devil!" exclaimed Tuttle. "You don't mean to give her this patent?"

"Well, I don't know," said the Governor-General.

"But I won't let her use my machinery!"

"Of course not," was the reply. "But you see, it seems to me purely a matter of form. If we give her this patent, it will satisfy all the rest. They will say we are enforcing the laws impartially; everybody has a fair chance—rich and poor are equal in the eyes of the law—and all that sort of thing, you know. But as a matter of fact, what good will it do her? She can't use your machinery; and she couldn't make the food tablets without stealing your formula. In the meantime, she has to go on making the food tablets for us in the old way. All we have to do is to sit tight, and in the end she'll have to sell us her invention."

" Sell it! " cried Tuttle. " You go to blazes! What do you think I'm goin' to pay her? "

" My dear fellow," laughed the Governor-General, " you wouldn't need to pay her very much. I'm not advising you to pay her a royalty, you understand—just simply some cash tablets."

And so it was arranged. To the great delight of Mrs. Lumley-Gotham her patent was issued in due form. Needless to say, her fellow wage slaves envied her good fortune. But they had to admit that this wonderful new civilization was giving everybody a square deal.

But alas for Mrs. Lumley-Gotham's hopes of leisure and luxury! With childish trustfulness she set to work to manufacture food tablets with the new machine, when suddenly

she was served with an injunction issued by
the Governor-General upon the application of
the President of the Amalgamated Food
Tablets Companies, Limited. She was tied
hand and foot—and moreover she had hanging
over her a heavy bill for court proceedings,
and a damage suit by holders of the original
patents!

She had to go to Tuttle for terms. When
she heard his offer : three food tablets a week
for the next six weeks, in exchange for the
full title to her invention, she laughed in his
face. She went away vowing that the tablets
would be prepared in the old way for ever
before she would accept such terms.

But alas for the unfortunate inventress!
She, the Mistress of Society, Mrs. Viviana
Athelstan de Smithkins Lumley-Gotham, was
now suddenly to realize the fate of the
proletarian, who has only his labour power to
sell, and has nothing to lose but his chains!
Three days the great capitalist waited for her
answer, and then she received notice that
unless his terms were accepted within three
days more, the wages of labour for cooking
and preparing the tablets would be cut twelve
and one-half per cent.—which would mean,

in plain, brutal language, that Mrs. Lumley-Gotham would be pledged to work two hours longer per day for the eight food tablets which were necessary to sustain her life!

Many indeed, were the lamentations, and direful were the threats that were made. The discontent became so great that it was necessary for the Governor-General to interfere. He read a few statutes on the subject of sedition and disrespect for the flag; and the Lord Bishop held special services, and preached a sermon on the subject of law and order, which exceeded in eloquence and definiteness anything which had ever emanated from the Consolidated Church of the Western Hemisphere in the days before the cataclysm.

In the end, of course, Mrs. Lumley-Gotham capitulated, and sold her invention for six hours' rest a week for six weeks. But it was with a heart full of bitterness and rage that she went back to work; and then it was that a new and terrible idea first had its birth in this new society. The form in which it reached the authorities was a report carried by the Lord Bishop, to the effect that Mrs. Lumley-Gotham had been heard to say that she would go back to work with her mind made up to make it dangerous for any capitalist to eat the food which she had prepared. So now a dread word began to be whispered through the corridors of the Consolidated Hotel. Sabotage!

Such evils do not come singly into the world. Those who are familiar with the economic interpretation of history will understand that under the highly organized system of exploitation which had now come to prevail, all the manifold evils of modern civilization would necessarily make their appearance. There was, for example, the dreadful phenomenon which social workers know as "industrial drinking." One Saturday night de Puyster went off on a spree, and on Sunday morning it was necessary for the Lord Bishop of Harlem to preach a sermon against intemperance, and to threaten legislation against bootleggers.

The Bishop wanted to go further, and found an Anti-Saloon League, receiving a contribution of food tablets as President thereof. After this point was made clear, Tuttle concluded suddenly that he believed in local option in such matters—if the working man drank on Sunday, he could go hungry on Monday, and be damned to him. And when the Bishop argued that this would result in inefficiency of labour, Tuttle replied that he didn't care a hang about inefficiency of labour. "Since Mrs. Lumley-Gotham got that new process," said he, "we can make all the food tablets we need in a few hours, and I have to think how to keep your people busy the rest of the time."

"Ah, me!" said the Bishop, shaking his head sadly. "If only you believed in the higher life, and would devote your wealth to the betterment of your fellow men!"

"In other words," said Tuttle, sarcastically, "if I would make the rest of them work harder in order that you might stop working!" So the Bishop went back to chopping furniture with a sorrowful heart.

Soon afterward there appeared another and still more dreadful phenomenon in society— that of crime. We should like to spare the reader's feelings, but the matter has deep social significance, and so the painful story must be told. Strange as it may seem, the person who departed from the paths of virtue was none other than the former Mistress of Society. Mrs. Viviana Athelstan de Smithkins Lumley-Gotham, forgetting the traditions of her race, forgetting all that she owed to the memory of her ancestors, the example which she must set to posterity—forgetting everything, in her avarice, envy and baffled hate—Mrs. Lumley-Gotham became a thief!

For some time there was no suspicion. She was working hard, and it was but natural that she should become exhausted and complain of headaches. She would take to her bed for half a day, and all unsuspecting, the Lord Bishop would bring her spiritual consolation, and de Puyster would come for the latest bulletins as to her condition, to be furnished to the Universal Press Association. But, after the way of all criminals, Mrs. Lumley-Gotham grew bolder; she stayed in bed whole days at a time—she stayed so long as to disorganize the machinery of production, and to cause a scarcity of the food tablets supply. And all the while, in spite of illness and lack of food, she grew no thinner; in fact, she looked better in health than before.

So at last the suspicions of the President of

the Amalgamated Food Tablets Companies, Limited, were excited, and he appealed to the Government. There was a consultation, after which appeared a new development in industrial life, one of the most sinister of the products of capitalistic evolution—the labour spy. The person who was selected to play this unlovely rôle was our unhappy friend, de Puyster. You will understand how this came about when you recall that he had fallen into the snares of the demon rum. He was tempted; and for the sum of one food tablet per day, he consented to keep watch upon Mrs. Lumley-Gotham.

At first he learned nothing, and there was discontent on the part of his employers, and threats to discharge him. But it was a difficult situation, because those in authority realized that if he were discharged, he might publish information as to the secret plans of the Government. So his salary was continued; and at last he came in great excitement with the statement that he had observed Mrs. Lumley-Gotham slip her hand under her pillow, and take out a food tablet and swallow it. She was not sick at all; she was stealing! So came the greatest scandal which ever had shaken society in the Consolidated Hotel. The Governor-General acted promptly. The grand jury, consisting of Tuttle, was convened, and a warrant was issued for the search of Mrs. Viviana Athelstan de Smithkins Lumley-Gotham's private dwelling. With this the Governor-General, the grand jury and the witnesses for the prosecution repaired to the rooms of the suspected person.

And then a storm broke. " What? " cried Mrs. Lumley-Gotham, hastily rolling herself up in her bedclothes. " You dare to come into my room! "

" Where did you get them tablets? " demanded Tuttle.

But the Governor-General put out his hand with a stern gesture. " Mr. Tuttle," he said, " you will kindly permit the constituted authority to deal with this matter."

" Granville," cried Mrs. Lumley-Gotham, " you get out of my room! "

Said the Governor-General, " This is an extremely painful ˙duty, but it must be performed."

Said Mrs. Lumley-Gotham, " What the devil are you talking about? " We apologize for this language, but the Mistress of Society was a personage accustomed to have her own way.

"What I mean," said the Governor-General, " is that we must search your room, and also your person, in order to find the food tablets which you have stolen."

"I? Stolen?" shrieked Mrs. Lumley-Gotham, furiously. "You dare——"

But at this moment de Puyster, from his place of safety behind the Governor-General, pointed an eager finger, crying, "There's a tablet now!"

Mrs. Lumley-Gotham made a wild grab to conceal the fatal object, but Tuttle was quicker. He seized her by the arm. She turned upon him like a tigress and planted upon his cheek a smack which might have been heard through all the corridors, if there had been anyone to hear. He recoiled, but still clung to her wrist; and let us be thankful that good society was not present to see Mrs. Viviana Athelstan de Smithkins Lumley-Gotham, clad only in her night-gown, engaged in a free fight with her head butler!

"Hold her, confound you!" shrieked Tuttle, after she had got her fingers twisted in his hair. " What are you the Governor-General for? "

" Well, really," said the Governor-General, smiling urbanely, " it seems to me this is a case where the business man might be expected to employ his own private detectives. Catch her hands, de Puyster ! "

Mrs. Lumley-Gotham turned upon the society reporter. " You wretch ! " she shouted. " You dare ! " And with her one free hand she made a swipe at de Puyster, which caused him to leap across the room.

Hearing her screams, the Lord Bishop now came in on the run; but spiritual offices proved utterly unavailing. A little later Lumley-Gotham himself appeared in the doorway. He was ordered, in his capacity as a citizen, to assist in maintaining the supremacy of the law; also, in his capacity as husband he was ordered to rescue his wife from a gang of ruffians. He settled the matter by fleeing from the scene.

The struggle ended at last, because Mrs. Lumley-Gotham suddenly remembered that it was her head butler with whom she was struggling. She drew herself up, haughtily, declaring, " You have the brute force; I scorn to struggle with you, ruffian! Take your hands off, and tell me what you want."

"I want to know where you got them tablets?" said Tuttle.

"What tablets?" she cried.

"The ones you've got under your pillow."

"I have no tablets under my pillow, nor anywhere else."

Tuttle sprang to the bed and dragged the pillow aside, disclosing a half-dozen of the tell-tale objects. "What have you got to say to that?" he cried.

Mrs. Lumley-Gotham looked at him as haughtily as an old lady can look when she has a torn night-gown, and her few remaining grey hairs straggling over her face. "If there are tablets there," she said, "I know nothing about them. Probably they were put there by some villain who wished to make trouble for me." And she turned upon de Puyster, who cringed. "What more likely than that they were put there by your labour spy?"

And so began one of the most famous legal trials in history—a trial which convulsed the world for many days, which divided society into two opposing camps, and which, as all students agree, was the greatest factor in bringing clearly into evidence the lines of the class-struggle. The truth about the matter has never really been decided; impartial historians still dispute about the probabilities, and quote the evidence in detail. Just how sick was Mrs. Lumley-Gotham? What was the likelihood of her illness being feigned? Just what opportunities did she have to steal food tablets? How much truth was there in the reports attributing to her incendiary and criminal utterances?

There was, for instance, the old story of the sale of her patent. It was known that she was very bitter about it, considering that she had been robbed. What was the likelihood of this bitterness having led her to yield to the temptation of crime? And then, on the other hand, there was the question of de Puyster and his character. What opportunities had he had to steal tablets? Just how much work had he done, and how much leisure had he earned by his services as a spy? What was the moral character of a man who was willing to sell out his fellows and betray his class? Would not such a man be willing to perjure himself?

Furious were the arguments over these questions, and bitter the denunciation hurled back and forth between the opposing camps. For weeks there was no other subject of conversation. There were parades and demonstrations—and so many threats of disorder that the authorities were driven to extreme measures. The talk of calling out the militia to preserve order was replied to by an anti-militarist propaganda. Just how far would it be possible to trust the troops in an emergency?

That there was difficulty in finding an impartial jury may readily be believed. When it was announced that the jury was to consist of Tuttle, there were many protests, and the authorities had to threaten stern repression, in case the preaching of disrespect for the judiciary did not cease. Belief in the courts, said the Governor-General, was the very foundation of civilized society; and agitators and fomentors of class hatred must somehow be made to realize the sanctity of law.

Mrs. Lumley-Gotham refused to employ counsel. She defended herself, and the ability and zeal which she displayed won the admiration even of her opponents. For nearly a week the hearings lasted, ably presided over by the Governor-General, in his capacity of Judge-Advocate. We will content ourselves here with the brief statement that the trial resulted in a verdict of guilty, and that Mrs. Lumley-Gotham was sentenced to thirty days' hard labour in the kitchen.

The sentence the prisoner received with what de Puyster's newspaper described as " disgraceful levity." In fact, she laughed in the face of the court, declaring that she had already been sentenced to hard labour in the kitchen for life by the industrial system then prevailing. To this the judge replied that if her unseemly conduct continued, he would alter the sentence to thirty days' solitary confinement upon bread and water. The prisoner called him a name which the press of the next morning did not print; she declared that she would refuse to serve her sentence, but that immediately upon her incarceration she would begin a hunger strike. At this her followers set up a wild cheer, and the judge ordered the court-room cleared.

Just what might have been the outcome of this intense situation, no one can say, for the next day there followed evidence so sensational as to give an entirely new turn to the course of events. That same evening an appalling discovery was made by the President of the Amalgamated Food Tablets Companies, Limited. De Puyster, the labour spy, the sole witness as to the iniquities of Mrs. Lumley-Gotham, was discovered endeavouring to make away with the box of food tablets which had been found under the pillow of the prisoner, and which had been filed as an exhibit at the trial. That this was a terrible blow to the prosecution need hardly be stated. The discovery, as it chanced, was made in the hearing of the prisoner and amidst the wildest rejoicings on the part of the revolutionary element, the case was reopened, and the defendant was acquitted—while the guilty labour spy was sentenced to receive a beating from the infuriated capitalist whom he had made ridiculous!

The agitation subsided for a time, and industry resumed its normal course. But never again could there be in this society the peace and unity of feeling of the old days. The effect of the disturbance had been to develop class consciousness; and now, throughout all the activities of life, whether industrial or social, one observed signs of ill-feeling. For example, the working class refused to associate with the hated spy. It was in vain that the Governor-General in his state papers expatiated upon the community of interest between capital and labour; it was in vain that the Lord Bishop preached eloquently upon Christian charity and forgiveness. De Puyster was a pariah to his own class.

Confidence had received a shock, from which it did not quickly recover. The working class found in the food factory daily evidence of suspicion, and humiliating reminders of their servile state. The capitalist moved his belongings into the factory and slept there by night. He was always prowling about by day, and when the last stage of the tablet-making process was reached, he was on hand, watching with hawk-like eyes the counting of the product.

Meantime a process of speeding up was developing. Each time the tablets were made, the workers were naturally more familiar with the whole work. They were able to make larger batches of tablets, and there was less risk of batches being spoiled. Presently this

led to new embarrassment; a new peril lifted
its head to confront the exploited workers—
the peril of over-production. Crises and
panics, with the unemployment and misery
which followed in their turn!

You can see very easily how it happened.
They produced all the tablets which Tuttle
and the Governor-General could eat; they
produced all they were allowed for themselves;
still there was a surplus. This surplus was
inconvenient, because Tuttle had to carry it
around with him all the time; there was no
place to lock it up, and he could trust no one
to mount guard over it. So, when this
burden came to be too inconvenient, naturally
the idea occurred to him to close down his
factory for a while.

But then arose the problem; what should
he do with his working people in the meantime? Should he continue to feed them with
tablets and let them live in idleness? If such
an idea has ever occurred to a business man, it
must have been in some part of the world not
yet discovered by explorers, and not written
up by the historians of industrial evolution.

As soon as the danger began to be realized,
the Lord Bishop of Harlem, in his character

of social mediator, thought of a solution, and
went to consult the authorities.   This state of
prosperity, he said, left a wonderful opportunity for the higher life to be developed.
Let the church now be endowed more
generously, so that the community might
turn a part of its efforts to spiritual things.

" In other words," said Tuttle, sarcastically,
" let you eat up the surplus tablets !   Is that
it ? "

" Ahem ! " said the Lord Bishop.   " If you
choose to phrase it in that unsympathetic
way——"

He turned to the Government.   Perhaps it
was true, he said, that the Government had
no funds; but that difficulty could easily be
remedied.   Let it tax the profits of corpora-
tions, and devote the proceeds to the support
of the higher life.   Whereupon—who can
describe the outburst of protest on the part
of outraged capital?   Had ever such a revolutionary proposal been heard of?   A tax upon
industry and thrift—and for the support of
superstition and prelatry !

" I am putting this thing to you in a
practical way," the Bishop persisted, " a way
that will appeal to the business man who wants

to see results. I tell you you can't get along without the church—without someone to teach obedience and respect for authority to your working class."

"Humph!" sneered the capitalist. "Much good your preaching has done! Look at this affair we've just passed through. What did you have to say about it?"

"Surely," said the Bishop, "you could not expect the church to take part in such political controversy. If the dignity of religion is to be maintained——"

"If the dignity of religion is to be maintained," snapped Tuttle, "you've got to loaf round all day looking solemn and putting on fat. Well, let me tell you the day has passed when you can work that kind of racket!"

The Bishop struggled to keep his temper. "Tell me this," he asked, "what do you plan to do?"

"I'll do the obvious thing," was the answer, "the thing that every business man does when he has a surplus stock on hand. I'll close down my factory until I've got rid of it."

"But then," cried the Bishop, "what will your working people do?"

" I don't know what they'll do. Let them shift for themselves."

" And you expect them to stand for that? "

" Stand for it? What do you mean? What else can they do? "

" They will protest."

" They can protest till they're black in the face—what do I care? "

" But, Mr. Tuttle," argued the Bishop, in excitement, " you will have a revolution on your hands! "

The other stared at him. " What kind of talk is this from a Bishop of the church? " he cried. " I thought you didn't meddle in politics."

The prelate turned upon the Governor-General. " Your Excellency," he cried, " will you stand for such a thing as that? "

" But," replied His Excellency, " what can I do? Mr. Tuttle is within his rights, and I am sworn to protect property and enforce the law."

There was a pause. His voice trembling slightly, the Bishop inquired, " Do I understand that this proposed stoppage of the food supply——"

" By which," interrupted Tuttle, " you

mean the closing down of the factory on account of lack of orders? "

" Do I understand," continued the other, " that this applies to me as well as to common labourers? "

" Why," was the response, " you'll have your Sunday supply of tablets, of course."

" But what am I to do on other days? " cried the amazed Bishop.

Tuttle shrugged his shoulders.

" But I am willing to work for my bread," persisted the other.

" I have no work for you," was the reply.

The other turned again to the Governor-General. " Your Excellency," he said, " I wish to ask you a question."

" Well? " inquired Granville.

" I want to know what is a man to do who is starving and can't find work? "

Whereupon His Excellency shrugged his shoulders. " God knows," said he. And thus ended the interview.

The reader will perceive that he has come to the beginning of a momentous development, destined to attract much attention from historians—the awakening of revolutionary sentiment in the church. Hitherto this great institution had been accounted one of the bulwarks of conservatism; but now the change began. The Lord Bishop of Harlem went out from this interview complaining bitterly, and presently it reached the ears of the constituted authorities that he had been seen in an assembly of revolutionary agitators. A day or two later, when the Amalgamated Food Tablets Companies, Limited, announced a shut-down of its factories for one week, the Bishop arose in his pulpit and preached a sermon upon the subject of the unemployed problem which created a terrific sensation in the community. The result was that the Bishop was cited to appear before the Governor-General, and without even the formalities of a hearing was deprived of his office, and all its perquisites, emoluments, privileges and immunities.

Which, of course, added fuel to the flame of discontent. The Bishop justified the worst suspicions of the ruling class by betaking himself to the meeting-place of the agitators, and there making an incendiary speech. He was followed by a notorious woman agitator, who had but recently been released from prison, and was under constant surveillance by the

police. There has always been dispute as
to what was said at this meeting, for
no representative of the Government was
admitted—a circumstance which led the
authorities later to call it a secret gathering
of conspirators. It is acknowledged, however, that at this meeting the former social
leader, Mrs. Viviana Athelstan de Smithkins
Lumley-Gotham, brought forward a new idea
—that of revolutionary industrial unionism.

" We have worked for the capitalist," said
the speaker, " and we have produced wealth
—much wealth. But this wealth belongs to
him, and not to us. We produced it—but
now we are turned out to starve, while he riots
in luxury and fattens in slothful ease. Let
us put an end to this diabolical system,
whereby we are deprived of the products of
our labour ! Let us organize, fellow-workers ;
let us make a common cause against this
enemy ! No matter what may be the nature
of our work, whether we have charge of the
fuel supply, whether we stir the kettles, or
transport the raw materials of the food tablets,
let the whole labour-force which has to do
with this work, organize itself into one big
union ! Let us vote together and strike

together, let us proclaim the supremacy of the working class and the end of exploitation! "

Mrs. Lumley-Gotham had risen to a great height of eloquence. " Working men of all countries unite! " she proclaimed. " You have nothing to lose but your chains, you have a world to gain! "

Needless to say, the report of this meeting brought consternation to the propertied classes. The Government set on foot an investigation at once; but the action was too late, for already the agitators had succeeded in inflaming the workers beyond the point where they could be controlled. The work of organizing the union was quickly completed, and the leaders proceeded at once to declare a strike. To the consternation of the Governor-General the announcement was made that they refused to have anything to do with him, but would treat only with the President of the Amalgamated Food Tablets Companies, Limited. Their demand was for an eight-hour day and a minimum wage of eight food tablets for every twenty-four hours, including Sundays. They declared that their strike would continue until these demands were granted; and to the amazement of the authorities they proceeded up and down the corridors of the Consolidated Hotel, cheering madly and singing the Internationale, the Marseillaise and other revolutionary songs of the old era. Also—a still more dreadful sign —they were waving aloft a blood-red banner, bearing three letters which brought terror to the hearts of all defenders of law and order—I.W.W.

There was a conference lasting several hours between the Governor-General and the President of the Amalgamated Food Tablets Companies, Limited. They sat barricaded in the kitchen, mounting guard over the food supply. They were alone as representatives of law and order; for in the revolutionary fervour old scores had been wiped out, and even de Puyster, the labour spy, had become a union man. Also Lumley-Gotham himself had joined the strike—although it was claimed that this was the result of intimidation. Rumour had it that the old man, a would-be strike-breaker, had been waylaid in the corridor, and severely beaten by a woman agitator, his wife.

" What are we going to do? " demanded Tuttle.

" I don't know," said the Governor-General. " Let them go, I suppose. Let them starve until they get tired of the game."

" But in the meantime, what are we to do? "

" How many tablets have we? " demanded Granville.

" A little over four hundred," was the reply.

" Something under four weeks' supply," mused the Governor-General. " They will never hold out that long, especially now that they have acquired the taste."

" But, confound it," exclaimed Tuttle, " what are we going to do about the rest of the work? "

The President of the Amalgamated Food Tablets Companies, Limited, had got so fat that it was hard for him to get out of his chair without help.

" We shall have to make out," said the Governor-General. " What else can we do? "

" I know what we ought to do," snapped the other, " get some of them people and make 'em work! "

" But we can't! " said the Governor-

General. " They are perfectly within their rights."

" Oh, hell ! " exclaimed the other. " Cut out that rot ! I say I want them people to come back. And what's more, I'll go out pretty soon and collar some of 'em and smash their faces in if they don't behave themselves."

" Of course," said the Governor-General, " you can try if you want to—but you know we have been living like gentlemen, recently."

" Well, I'll soon stop being a gentleman, if this here strike goes on."

They talked things over that day, and they talked them over for several days more. The ranks of the strikers continued unbroken. But they knew that there was one, at least, who must be wavering—poor Lumley-Gotham himself, who had always before him the prediction of his physicians that he would die if he tried to live upon anything but food tablets. Surely he must be eager to return to his job of general handy-man ! If only they could get him, they could hold out against the strike for ever, because in the emergency he could be made to produce as many tablets as were necessary for three. How to get him —that was the problem !

A week passed; two weeks passed; and Tuttle having to do his own work, got much thinner and began to feel more active, as well as more angry. One night, without saying anything to the Governor-General, he sallied forth and sought out the store-rooms of the Amalgamated Groceries Company, where the strikers had opened their headquarters. Prowling about in these rooms in the darkness, Tuttle at last espied Lumley-Gotham himself, and gave a low whistle to make his presence known. He beckoned to the terrified old man and stole away to a remote room, where behind barred doors there was a whispered conference.

The purport of it may be easily guessed. Tuttle found that the other was eager to return to work. He was not afraid of the title of " scab "; he was only afraid of physical violence from his fellow-strikers, and if he could be assured of adequate police protection —especially against women agitators—he would be willing to come to the Consolidated Hotel.

Said Tuttle, " You need never go out of the kitchen; and if any of them strikers tries to get near you—well, you just leave that to

me and the Governor-General." So that
very night the old man fled. And in the
morning the dismayed strikers realized that
they were in the hands of their exploiters!

Here again we reach a portion of our history
which is a subject of much dispute. Just how
did violence begin, and who was to blame for
it? Was it true, as the Governor-General
claimed, that the strike leaders, while they
disclaimed violence in their speeches, were
secretly encouraging it and supporting it?
Was it true that at their meetings there were
threats of wrecking machinery, and even of
putting poison in the food tablets, should the
strike be lost? Or, on the other hand, was
it true, as the strikers claimed, that they
attempted only peaceful picketing, and that
all the violence was on the side of the
authorities?

However this might be, the war was now
on in deadly earnest. To begin with, Mrs.
Lumley-Gotham appeared, demanding an
interview with the scab, upon the wholly
preposterous ground that he was her husband.
And then came the President of the Wood-
chopper's union, the unfrocked Lord Bishop
of Harlem. When the request of this pair

had been denied, they set up the claim that Lumley-Gotham himself had been kidnapped by violence, and they served upon the Judge-Advocate a demand for a writ of habeas corpus. This request also was refused.

What followed after that is a matter of dispute, owing mainly to the fact that the representative of the press was excluded from the meeting. The contention of the strikers was that they protested against this star-chamber proceeding, and declared their intention to continue the strike to the bitter end. On the other hand, the authorities maintained that the strikers uttered seditious threats; that they laid themselves open to a score of charges—of which blasphemy, contempt of court, high treason, and *lese majesté* were the least.

The conference broke up, and the strike committee went away, foiled of its purpose. Another two weeks passed, during which the authorities stood pat, and during which the I.W.W. members ate the canned food from the store-rooms of the Amalgamated Groceries Company, and wrestled with the torments of indigestion and the spectre of ptomaines and anhydrous sodium sulphite. So at last matters came to a head. Mrs. Lumley-Gotham became seriously ill, and she made one last desperate attempt to appeal to the better feelings of the scab, her husband. She wrote a letter in which she implored him to come out on strike again—and in which incidentally she expressed her opinion concerning capitalists and hireling politicians. This letter she entrusted to de Puyster, who undertook to get into the Consolidated Hotel by one of the numerous entrances, and to dangle the letter by a string in front of the window where Lumley-Gotham was known to be at work.

It was a brilliant scheme, but alas, it happened that Tuttle, prowling about the building, came upon de Puyster, overhauled him, and took away the note. The unhappy wretch was first clubbed into submission, and then led before the Governor-General, who immediately ordered him into close confinement, upon a variety of charges, which included breaking in and entering, conspiracy, and the publishing and circulating of seditious utterances.

After further consideration of the note, and the discussion of ways and means, the

President of the Amalgamated Food Tablets Companies, Limited, was sworn in as deputy sheriff and was sent out with warrants ordering the arrest of Mrs. Viviana Athelstan de Smithkins Lumley-Gotham on a charge of incitement to violence, and of His Grace, the Lord Bishop of Harlem, upon a charge of speaking disrespectfully of the flag. These warrants were duly served, with the result that the strike came to an end.

The trials of the leaders were held next day. Mrs. Lumley-Gotham was ordered into solitary confinement, under close guard, until her health was restored and she was able to work again; while de Puyster and the Lord Bishop were sentenced each to seven years of hard labour in the food factory. So came to an end the industrial union agitation, and the dreadful spectre of the I.W.W. was laid.

Those who claim that capitalism is simply a disguised form of Slavery would have found support for their arguments in the conditions which prevailed after the breaking of the strike. At the Consolidated Hotel there was no longer any pretence of liberty or justice. Mrs. Lumley-Gotham, the Lord Bishop and de Puyster were nominally convict labourers, but their position was precisely the same as it had been when they were Tuttle's slaves. They had to work as long as they were told to work, and under any conditions, and they received in return only as much food as their master considered necessary to keep them in condition. They had no longer any rights, and at the least offence were liable to brutal punishment.

Nor was the condition of Lumley-Gotham himself, who was considered to be a free labourer, much better. He got no reward, nor even thanks, for his help in breaking the strike. He was liable to be beaten just as severely when Tuttle was drunk; nor was anything to be gained by appealing to the law, for the Governor-General had withdrawn more and more to himself, having no taste for the rattle of chains and the wielding of whips.

In fact, the only thing that saved the revolutionists was the circumstance that after the strike was broken, Tuttle immediately proceeded to grow fat again. Very soon he got so fat that he was not equal to the exertion of beating them, even when drunk;

and so, little by little, the watch over the prisoners was relaxed and they began to take courage and dream of fresh resistance.

Mrs. Lumley-Gotham recovered her health, and immediately set to work planning a convict mutiny. Between herself and the Lord Bishop there had developed a spirit of comradeship, of mutual trust, such as can be generated only by the fires of persecution. All day long, as they went about their tasks in the kitchen, dragging their clanking chains behind them, they were on the look out for moments when they could exchange a few whispered words.

The reader will no doubt by this time have perceived that the former Mistress of Society was a personage of no common powers. Thrown upon her own resources by an unkind fate, she had exhibited resourcefulness, courage and determination. Now by suffering and persecution her will had been tempered to steel. She was undaunted in spirit—and after the example of many of the great souls of history, she had found time to think while she was in prison.

Bit by bit the Lord Bishop gathered her ideas—and most startling ideas they were, to have sprung up in the mind of the wife of the owner of the greater part of the Western Hemisphere! She had studied the whole problem carefully, and had come to the conclusion that it was her historic destiny to put an end to the tyranny of the capitalist regime. She might have poisoned Tuttle, her master; she might have thrust a knife into his huge fat carcass when he lay asleep; but she had decided not to do anything like this, because her mind had grasped the fundamental idea that crime breeds crime, and that civilization cannot be built upon the motto, "An eye for an eye."

"It has become perfectly clear to me," she said to the Bishop, "that the wrong in our present arrangements lies in the fact that Tuttle claims to own the food tablets machinery. So he has us in his power, and we have to work for him on his own terms. If we should overthrow him, and permit any other person to own the machinery, that person in turn would make slaves of the rest, and we should have the old wickedness and misery all over again. What we must do is to make up our minds once for all that no individual is to be allowed to own the food machinery; the food machinery must be the property of the whole community, and those who use it must receive the full value of what they produce. So there will be justice and order, and no man will be able to live in idleness upon the product of another man's toil."

This conversation occurred one evening in the passage-way, when the two had chanced to meet—Mrs. Lumley-Gotham carrying a kettle full of boiling water and the Lord Bishop an armful of chopped furniture. As the latter took in the full import of her words, he nearly dropped his load. "My dear lady," he whispered, " do you realize what it is that you are talking to me? "

Said the other, "What do you mean? "

" It's Socialism! " exclaimed the Bishop.

For a moment Mrs. Lumley-Gotham shared his emotion of fear. But quickly she got herself together. " Call it Socialism," she said, " or call it Anarchism—I don't care. What I know is that it's common sense, and nobody will ever be able to fool me about it again. I am ashamed of myself that I have never been able to see it all these years, when I was a parasite, a spendthrift idler. Go on, carry in your wood before Tuttle sees us talking. But put your mind to work and figure out how we can get these chains off."

The next time the Bishop went out for wood, he visited a hardware store and possessed himself of a couple of files; and that night, while Tuttle was asleep, he and Mrs. Lumley-Gotham filed the chains which fastened them in their separate cells. It took them but a short time longer to find the room where de Puyster was confined, and to set him free; and then the three breathless conspirators crept on tiptoe down the corridors and made their way to the street.

Under the stars the Lord Bishop of Harlem stopped and stared at Mrs. Lumley-Gotham, whispering, " Aren't you going to take your husband, also? "

" What? " exclaimed the woman. " That traitor? that cowardly wretch? "

" But," stammered the Bishop, " we *must* take him! "

" Why must we? If we let him know what we are doing, he would betray us to Tuttle."

" I know," exclaimed the other, " but don't you see, dear lady? We can't possibly go away like this—stop and realize it for a moment!"

"I don't know what you are talking about," said his companion.

"You are Mrs. Lumley-Gotham, are you not?"

"Of course."

"And I am the Lord Bishop of Harlem. And we two steal out of our hotel in the dead of night, take an automobile and ride away— no one knows where—and with no one but a newspaper reporter to chaperon us! Why, Mrs. Lumley-Gotham, imagine the scandal!"

The Mistress of Society clenched her hands and replied, "I don't care anything about the scandal! I want to get away from Tuttle!"

"But, my dear lady," pleaded the other, "I can't permit it! Even if you are willing to take the risk, I have to consider what I owe to my exalted office. Why, if the newspapers were to get hold of such a story——"

"I will see that they don't," broke in de Puyster. "I will use my influence——"

"But the story would leak out," persisted the Bishop. "Only see! You propose to come out before the world as a Socialist; and don't you know the first thing that everybody says about Socialists? I can't bring myself to pronounce the dreadful words——"

" You mean ' free love '? " demanded Mrs. Lumley-Gotham, who had lost that fine delicacy of feeling which had been her distinction in the old days.

" Y-yes," stammered the Bishop. " And consider—here is Socialism breaking up the home. Don't you see what a black eye you would give the movement at the very outset? "

" A plague upon the movement! Don't you see there is nobody to join it but us? "

The Lord Bishop's answer was to seat himself upon the steps of the Consolidated Hotel. " I can't answer your argument," he said, " but this I know very clearly, there is nothing in the world that could persuade me to run away at night in an automobile with another man's wife."

So at last, seeing he was not to be moved, Mrs. Lumley-Gotham demanded what must be done.

" We must take Lumley-Gotham along," said the Bishop.

" But we dare not tell him."

" We don't need to tell him. Let's take him by force."

And so at last it was decided. The three revolutionists crept along the corridors of the hotel once more. They opened softly the door of the room where Tuttle lay, like a snoring hippopotamus. They crept past him, and over into the corner where the timid strike-breaker made his bed. One seized his feet, another seized his arms, and a third clapped her hand over his mouth; and thus they bore him, wriggling and gasping with terror, out of the room and out of the hotel. In a nearby garage they found an automobile, and after tying him hand and foot, they deposited him on the floor and set out.

At the northern end of Manhattan Island, they hid in a garage until morning. They wrapped up their kidnapped chaperon in blankets, so that he might not suffer from the cold, and then they sat in a corner and talked over their plans. Whither should they fly?

It was Mrs. Lumley-Gotham who made the suggestion that carried the day. Up in the Pocantico Hills, the Lumley-Gotham country estate, was to be found a duplicate outfit of the food tablet machinery. It was the only place they knew of where this could be found; so obviously, here was their goal.

When dawn came, making it possible for them to find the road, they refreshed themselves with a supply of stolen food tablets, and then set out. How beautiful and wonderful seemed the country, after their long sojourn within marble halls. And how sweet was the sense of freedom, after having passed through all the stages of social evolution—through Slavery, Feudalism and Capitalism!

There were scores of bridges and roads leading from the city in every direction, so the chances of pursuit seemed almost nil. Therefore you can imagine their consternation, when, coming over a rise of ground, Mrs. Lumley-Gotham chanced to look behind her, and screamed. " There's an automobile following us ! "

" Impossible ! " cried the Lord Bishop, who was acting as chauffeur.

" But I see them ! Look ! Look ! " she said.

And de Puyster added, " I see them, too. There are two people in the car."

" They are after us ! " cried the woman, in a voice of grief. " We are lost ! "

" Faster!   Faster! " shouted de Puyster.
The Lord Bishop obeyed and the car leaped
ahead.

" Don't let them catch us! " exclaimed
Mrs. Lumley-Gotham.   " Let's die first! "
And that indeed seemed more likely, at the
rate the car whirled around the corners.   She
and de Puyster were kneeling in the seat,
gazing behind them.

The other car was no longer in sight.
There was a chance yet!   " Let's turn off one
of the side-roads," cried Mrs. Lumley-
Gotham.

The Lord Bishop answered nothing.   He
was staring ahead, every faculty tense with
concentration upon his task.   De Puyster
spoke for him.   " What good will it do to
turn off?   They have figured where we must
go—where the food machinery is."

" Oh,   sure   enough! "   exclaimed   Mrs.
Lumley-Gotham.   Then after a moment she
added, " And we can't live without the food
tablets! "   No one answered this terrible
remark—which was like a sentence of
doom.

They came over another rise of ground, and
there behind them they saw the car.   " They

are going faster! They are trying to catch us! Go! Go!" shouted Mrs. Lumley-Gotham.

They swept down a hill into a town. The street had many turns, and there were wagons and cars, where they had been left at the time of the cataclysm. So it was necessary to go slow.

But alas, they didn't go slow enough. Turning a corner there was a blockade in the street. The Bishop jammed down the emergency brake and swung the car off towards the sidewalk. It took the curbstone with a graceful leap, went over the sidewalk, knocked down an area railing, and went through a bakery window, after which it stopped. Nobody was hurt, at least not seriously; but they were all shaken up and bewildered, and by the time they had got themselves together and extracted themselves from the car and the bakery, the other car was in plain sight down the street.

"Into the house!" cried Mrs. Lumley-Gotham, wildly. "Let's hide!"

"Scatter!" cried the Lord Bishop. "Some of us can get away!"

They were about to obey this order, when

suddenly from the approaching car was
heard a woman's shrill voice, " Mother!
Mother! "

They stopped, and stood looking in amazement. " Mother! " shrieked the voice from
the approaching automobile. " Why don't
you wait for us? "

The occupants of the car were Eloise
Lumley-Gotham and Mr. Reginald Simpkins,
poet laureate of society!

The car drew up and stopped. " Mother,
why are you running away from us? " cried
Eloise.

" We were not running away from *you*,"
was the reply. " We were running away
from Tuttle."

Needless to say, neither Eloise nor Reggie
required further reason. Reggie's person still
bore the scars he had received from his cruel
master. " Where is he? " cried Eloise,
gazing down the street in alarm.

" Here, jump in with us," cried Reggie.
" Let's go! "

" Quick! Quick! " added Eloise.

Mrs. Lumley-Gotham made haste to obey,
and the Bishop and de Puyster followed. The
car was going on, when suddenly from inside

the bakery a shrill, wailing voice was heard.
" Are you going to leave me behind? "

" Who's that? " cried Eloise.

" It is your father," was the reply from the
Lord Bishop. " Wait, I'll cut him loose."

Then up spoke Mrs. Lumley-Gotham.
" Do nothing of the kind. Come on! "

" But—but——" stammered the Bishop.
" What do you mean? "

" I mean that we don't need him any more.
My daughter can chaperon me now."

The others looked at her in amazement.
From the bakery came a shriek of terror.
" No, no! Don't leave me here! Have
mercy! Have mercy! "

" Mother, what's the matter? What do
you mean? " cried Eloise.

All stood waiting upon Mrs. Lumley-
Gotham. " He is a scab," she declared.
" He is unworthy of help——"

But she got no further. The voice of the
Lord Bishop was heard, in the solemn tones
which he reserved for professional purposes.
" Mrs. Lumley-Gotham, let me not hear such
inhuman sentiments proceeding from your
lips! Have you not told me that you desire
to inaugurate an age of brotherhood and co-

operation? Have you not told me that you desire to wipe away the stains of old evils and begin a new life? If that be true, let us begin with yon poor wretch, who was driven by weakness and fear to serve the vile purposes of Capitalism."

There was a silence, while all stood watching the angry woman. "Mrs. Lumley-Gotham," continued the Bishop, impressively, "in the name of the Co-operative Commonwealth which is to be, I adjure that you forgive that wretched strike-breaker, your husband. Let us witness here, in this great moment, an action that shall symbolize the beginning of the new order. Go yourself and untie the bands that bind the last wage slave, and bid him rise up a free and equal citizen of the Socialist State!"

Mrs. Lumley-Gotham could not resist the spell of this noble idea. As one in a trance, she moved across the street, and crawled into the automobile, and untied the cords which were bound around the wrists and ankles of Lumley-Gotham himself. The old man rose up and stretched himself, and a hush fell upon all the beholders, who knew that they were witnessing a scene which the historians and poets of the future would never grow weary of describing.

The party, now increased to six, proceeded upon their way. There was no longer any fear of pursuit, so there was time for explanations. Reggie and Eloise told the story of their escape from Tuttle, and how they had fled away to a town in New Jersey, where they had spent the summer. Now, dreading the approaching cold weather, they had decided to make their way to the country place in the Pocantico Hills. The poet laureate, it seemed, had found in the public library a treatise on electricity; he had been studying it diligently, and believed that he would be able to run the heating plant in the Lumley-Gotham home.

"How extraordinary!" exclaimed Mrs. Lumley-Gotham. "We were going there also!" And she went on to tell the tidings of their discovery of the food tablets. "How in the world have you managed to keep alive on canned food?" she asked.

"We haven't," Eloise replied. "We have been raising vegetables. Look!" And she lifted the robe which covered the bottom of the car, disclosing some garden truck. "We were taking it with us," she said. "And oh, mother, if you could have seen the funny times we had—trying to raise things! First, we planted our corn about a foot deep!"

"And we planted roasted peanuts and pickled olives!" laughed Reggie.

It was the first time our unhappy runaways had laughed for many a month. Their enjoyment was short-lived, however—for suddenly a dreadful idea flashed over Mrs. Lumley-Gotham. All these bucolic pursuits, these humours of domestic life—what horrors lay behind them? Her younger daughter, an heiress of the line of Lumley-Gotham, living all this time unchaperoned with a man! And a man of no particular social position—a mere poet!

"Why, Eloise!" she exclaimed. "What am I to understand? What——"

"What's the matter, mother?" inquired the girl.

"You—and—Mr. Simpkins——" (He became suddenly Mr. Simpkins in this trying moment.)

Suddenly Eloise caught her meaning. She flushed quickly. "Why, mother, you see—you see——"

A silence fell. Neither of them could speak. They had spoken too much already—in the presence of all the world! "Mother," burst out Eloise, with sudden vehemence, "what else could we do?"

"Hush, my child!" cried the mother.

"There was nobody—no clergyman—no one!"

"You should have come and found the Bishop," exclaimed the Mistress of Society.

"But there was Tuttle!" cried the girl. "We were in terror of him!"

"Mrs. Lumley-Gotham," pleaded the poet laureate, in distress of soul, "if you could see the scars on my arms! And on my back! And on my——"

Not even poetic licence could carry him further. There was a long silence. Suddenly the voice of the great lady was heard. "Mr. Simpkins, please stop this car."

"Stop the car?" echoed the poet. "Why——"

"Stop the car!" repeated the great lady, imperiously. And the command was obeyed.

She turned to His Grace, the Lord Bishop,

saying, " Will you please marry my daughter and Mr. Simpkins? "

Everybody was staring at her. The Lord Bishop was hardly able to comprehend the words. " What? Now? " he cried.

" Instantly ! " was the answer.

" But, mother, we don't want to stop now. The danger——"

" There is no danger compared with the danger of disgrace."

" But surely," broke in the poet, " when we have reached our destination——"

" Mr. Simpkins," said Mrs. Lumley-Gotham, in a freezing voice, " it seems to me that under the circumstances it ill becomes you to make objections."

" But, mother," persisted Eloise, " what harm can it do to wait until we stop? "

" Suppose," was the reply, " that we were to meet with another accident, and that Mr. Simpkins should be killed. What then would become of the honour of the line of Lumley-Gotham? How could we ever wipe out the blot upon our escutcheon? "

There was no answer to this.

The Mistress of Society demanded, " Bishop, will you marry my daughter and Mr. Simpkins at once?" And so, without further delay, seated there in the automobile, the Bishop pronounced the magic formula.

When this ceremony was over, when congratulations had been given and received, and all parties concerned had shaken hands, Mrs. Lumley-Gotham sought to exact a pledge of secrecy as to the past. But fortunately there was one person to whom the sensational circumstances afforded too great a temptation. Mr. Harold de Puyster, society reporter of the Universal Press Association, had a sense of the picturesque and the poetical so highly developed that he was moved to set down the story in his private diary—to which source posterity is indebted for this present account of the first marriage in the Co-operative Commonwealth.

The remainder of the trip was completed without incident. They came to the entrance to the estate, where to their surprise they found the huge bronze gates lying open— something which had not been known for more than a generation. But still greater surprise awaited them as the automobile made its way up the driveway, and emerged from the forest into sight of the palace which the Lumley-

Gothams had built for their summer home. Upon the smooth lawn in front of the main building, plainly visible, stood a woman!

Words cannot portray the consternation of the party. It had been six months since the catacylsm, and they had grown so used to seeing the world about them without inhabitants, that they were as much astonished as Robinson Crusoe when he discovered the footprints on the sands. Their first idea was that they had got to a place where the explosion had had no effect. But as they came nearer, they realized their mistake. The woman was Helen!

She had seen them, and now came forward to welcome them.

And then came Sarita and Billy, having heard the sounds of the automobile. What a scene there was—the embraces and handshakings and cries of delight! And such an endless string of reminiscences to be exchanged! No one would have thought that these two groups of people had parted after a violent dispute.

" How in the world did you know that we were here? " demanded Billy.

" We didn't know it," answered Mrs.

Lumley-Gotham. "We came here because it was the only place we knew where the food tablets could be manufactured."

"What?" cried Billy. "Have you learned to do that?" And so the whole story of the struggle with Tuttle and Granville had to be told.

"Oh, Helen," said her mother, "we have had such a dreadful time."

"You have concluded to forgive us?" inquired Helen.

"I will consent to the divorce," was the answer.

"And the Bishop?" inquired Billy, with a smile.

"The Bishop," answered Mrs. Lumley-Gotham, gravely, "has become a Socialist."

There was an awe-stricken silence after this announcement. Eloise looked dismayed; it suddenly occurred to her to doubt the validity of a marriage ceremony which had been performed by a Socialist Bishop.

"Are you a Socialist, too?" inquired Billy, looking at Mrs. Lumley-Gotham.

"I," said the great lady, proudly, "am an organizer of the I.W.W." Again there was silence, longer than before.

" Billy," said Mrs. Lumley-Gotham, at last, " we are in great distress, and we need help. We would like to join with you and start over again if you are willing.   But you must understand that we have very intense convictions, and that sooner than part with them, we will go our way and shift for ourselves.   The Bishop and de Puyster and myself have sworn to live and die by the principles of the social revolution.   We have the secret formula of the food tablets, and we understand how to run the machinery.   We might set ourselves up as capitalists, and go through the whole dreadful history of the class war again; but we have learned our lesson, and never more will we have anything to do with private property in the means of production.   If we join forces with you, the food formula and the machinery and everything else that we use must belong to the whole community, and everyone, both men and women, must have an equal say as to how it is managed.   Are you willing to agree to that? "

And Helen came and put her arms about her mother's neck.   " Mother, dear," she said, " we arranged all that the day after we got here.   Come up to the house and read the constitution of our Co-operative Commonwealth!"

It was the first day of May of the following year, and the inhabitants of the new community were celebrating the great international holiday at the Lumley-Gotham country estate.

It was sunset, and the vast stone buildings shone red. There was a party of merry-makers gathered on the lawn, which sloped down to Italian gardens, with a view of the Hudson river and hills in the distance. Reginald Simpkins and Eloise Lumley-Gotham were setting the supper table. The poet laureate wore soft flannels and sandals, and a loose tie of the most approved revolutionary colour; while the women also wore soft flannels and sandals—producing a Utopian effect. Indeed, the only person in the party whose costume contained any reminder of the past was de Puyster, the society reporter, who was occupied in distributing the third number of the "Pocantico Pioneer," of which he was editor, publisher, printer and newsagent.

A short distance removed from the others you might have seen Sarita Knickerbocker-Smythe, wearing bloomers, and seated under the shelter of a tree, keeping watch over a baby-carriage. This was Helen's baby—the first baby under the new dispensation. You may imagine what care they took of it, and how much excitement there was every time it had to be moved.

His Grace, the Lord Bishop of Harlem, was occupied in hanging Japanese lanterns for the evening's festivities, while Billy was bringing in a hamper of supplies for the feast. Reggie and Eloise were quarrelling—for you must not imagine that the magic formula which the Bishop had pronounced over them five or six months before had put an end to their tendency to argue with each other. Not even in the Co-operative Commonwealth do all the problems of matrimonial life stay solved!

One of the topics of dispute at present was the costume of Sarita Knickerbocker-Smythe, which was an innovation, and a continued cause of horror to Eloise. " My dear Sarita," she was protesting, " you might wear a skirt for the May-Day party at least."

To which Sarita answered, "What's the use, my dear? Everybody knows the worst by now." She peered in under the coverings of the carriage, exclaiming in a tone of voice which is known to all friends of babies, "He was a pitty-itty tootsie-wootsie."

Eloise left off the sorting of knives and forks. "Isn't he a perfect angel!"

"He is a itty-pitty angel!" said Sarita.

"He is a perfect image of Helen," said Eloise.

"Of Helen?" protested Reggie. "Why, he has Billy's nose!"

"Well," said Sarita, pouring oil on the matrimonial waters, "he has got a itty-pitty love of a nose, anyhow." And then, dangling a flower in front of the said nose, "He was his mamma's itty lamb!"

At this moment Helen entered, radiant and laughing, carrying an armful of flowers which she had been gathering in the gardens. She was clad in a graceful costume which might have come down from the days of Shakespeare's romantic comedies. "Who is spoiling my baby?" she demanded.

"Who isn't you might have asked," responded Sarita, who had taken the precious object in her arms and sat gazing at it.

"Ah, me," said Eloise, "what a wonderful thing is a baby!"

" The only baby in the world! " added Reggie.

It was curious to see the simplicity with which these two young folks discussed the subject of babies—the first, which had recently arrived, and the second, their own, which was expected. It was quite a contrast with the cynicism and smartness of the old life.

The community had had a reminder of the change that afternoon, for it chanced that Billy, while tinkering with some of the machinery of the estate, had opened the receiver of one of the pneumatic tubes, and had taken out a newspaper, a special extra of a New York evening paper on the day of the cataclysm. He produced the copy and they gathered about, gazing at it in wonder. The whole of the front page was given up to an account of how Guiseppe Scliapine had chopped up his sweetheart with an axe in the rear room of a Baxter Street tenement; the last page to an editorial upon the evils of smoking cigarettes in bed. Practically all the rest of the paper was devoted to an advance account of the great ball at the Pleasure Palace. They passed the sheets around and gazed at their pictures in costume, and the long accounts of the festivities written by their friend de Puyster.

" Let's hear it! " cried someone, and Billy read aloud : " ' The glorious strains of the Citizens' Alliance March now hailed the approach of the hostess of the occasion—Mrs. Viviana Athelstan de Smithkins Lumley-Gotham, to whose munificence society owes the existence of the great temple of hospitality, a temple preserved for ever from all contact with vulgar life, and dedicated to the service of those to whom God in His infinite wisdom has entrusted the care of the property interests of the country.' "

" Oh! Oh! Oh! " cried all.

" De Puyster's style was a trifle florid in those days," laughed Billy.

" Doesn't it seem strange? " agreed Eloise.

" What a dreadful world it was! " added Sarita.

" Just as a matter of curiosity," put in Helen, " I wonder if there is anybody who would go back if he had a chance? "

They stared at her in dismay. " Go back! " they cried.

" Think it over," said Helen. " It is interesting.

" You mean with everything the same as it used to be? " inquired Reggie.

" Yes," said she. " Would you, Bishop? "

" Well," said the Bishop, " I must confess that I occasionally have yearnings for—say, a broiled grouse with a bit of bacon. But everything? No, no! "

" Think of having to wear starched shirts! " cried Reggie.

" Think of having to dress half a dozen times a day! " cried Eloise.

" And wearing long robes! " cried the Bishop.

" And having to sign cheques! " exclaimed Lumley-Gotham himself.

" And corsets! " cried the Mistress of Society.

" And cigarettes and high-balls! " cried Sarita. " What unhappy creatures we were." She paused for a moment, and then continued, moralizing, " It wasn't our fault. There were forces that made us what we were, and we didn't understand. That is why, whenever I think of it, I feel sorry for

the two men we left behind in the city.
That is why I say we ought to try to redeem
them——"

Eloise interrupted. "Are you starting
that question again?"

"I have told you," Sarita answered. "I
will never let it rest. We owe both Granville
and Tuttle a chance to reform."

"We owe them nothing!" cried Eloise,
angrily. "There is absolutely nothing we
can do for them."

"We can offer them a pardon," persisted
the other. "We have no right to say that
any human being is hopeless, incapable of
better things——"

"It is all very well for you to talk," broke
in Reginald Simpkins. "You never had
Tuttle beat you."

"Tuttle is what we made him," answered
Sarita. "We brought him up to be a slave,
to minister to our idleness and vanity. How
can we blame him if he tried to turn the
tables upon us when he had a chance? But
I am not speaking of Tuttle alone. There
is Granville also."

"Granville is worse than Tuttle,"
exclaimed Mrs. Lumley-Gotham. "He is

an intellectual man, and should have known better."

"In our world," answered Sarita, "the corruption was worse among intellectual people than among the lower classes. Granville should be forgiven, too." She turned to the Lord Bishop. "Has your religion nothing to say for them?"

The Bishop hemmed. "Just what is it that you want me to do, Sarita?"

She paused a moment before answering. "Listen, friends," she began, "I have something important to tell you. You remember that yesterday I was away all day, and I told you that my automobile had broken down. Well, that is not true. What happened was I went to New York."

They stared at her in consternation. "To New York!"

"As you know, all winter long I have been thinking about the fate of those two wretched men. I made up my mind that I would wait no longer, that I would seek them out and give them a chance—at least the one whom I believed might be redeemed." She paused; you might have heard the buzzing of a fly in the silence that followed.

" Well? " asked Mrs. Lumley-Gotham, at last.

" I went to the city. I made my way on foot to the Consolidated Hotel, and entered quietly, and found the place where the food machinery was kept. For a long time I saw no one, but there were signs that someone had been there recently, and I continued my search, quietly and cautiously. And at last I came upon one of them."

Again there was silence. " Well? " inquired Billy, at last.

" It was Granville."

" What about him? "

" He and Tuttle had quarrelled over the right to use the machinery. Tuttle had insisted that he owned it, and had tried to make Granville do the work for both. They had had a fight, and Granville had been hurt —not seriously, but he had had to hide. Now for months he had been hunting for Tuttle, and Tuttle presumably was hunting for him —both of them armed and bent on murder."

Sarita paused. Her voice was trembling as she continued : " You cannot imagine the miserable plight Granville was in. All winter long he had had no fuel—he dared not build a fire, for fear of revealing his whereabouts to Tuttle. Neither dared use the food machinery for fear of assassination. They were living like animals, stalking each other day and night. Granville was ill—thoroughly worn out with it. So I persuaded him to come away—to come with me——"

There was a cry of consternation.

" He is here? " asked Billy. And Sarita nodded.

A long silence followed. " On what terms is he here? " demanded Mrs. Lumley-Gotham, the self-appointed guardian of the principles of the Co-operative Commonwealth.

" On no terms at all, at present," said Sarita. " It is for you to admit him if you are willing. He wishes to come on the same conditions as the rest of us. He will renounce his old titles of Secretary of State and Baron and Governor-General and will become plain Comrade Granville."

Silence followed, while the members of the community considered the proposition. " Will he do his share of the work? " inquired Eloise.

" He will," was the answer.

" What guarantee can we have of that? "

"The best of guarantees," was Sarita's reply. "I will attend to it."

"But how can you attend to it?" Eloise demanded.

To which the other answered, "The Lord Bishop of Harlem will put him in my power. He has agreed to marry me."

First they stared in amazement; then came a shout of laughter and acclamation. None of them had had the least idea of the situation —none, at least, save Helen, who had guessed the reason for Sarita's concern over the fate of the unhappy Governor-General.

She had hidden her lover away in one of the remoter buildings of the estate. Now at her call he emerged, emaciated, and seeming years older—but still the same Granville, mocking and serene.

"Friends," he remarked, "I have a humiliating statement to make—one that should make any man blush. I have, as you know, aspired to be an intellectual being. For a whole year I have striven to act upon my convictions, to withhold myself from entanglement with the victims of the moral sense. But alas—how shall I say it? I bow my head with shame, I heap ashes of

contrition upon myself as I utter the words
—but the truth remains. For several months
I have been—actually, ladies and gentlemen,
I have been finding myself lonely!"

No one spoke. They waited for him to
come to the point. "It is the life-force," he
said. "I feel in me its dreadful, tormenting
urge. It haunts me, it obsesses me, it drives
me mad with fury and shame. It has chosen
to take that most preposterous and humiliating of all forms. Think of it, my friends,
this is St. Erskine Granville who is making
the confession to you—it has taken the form
of a woman!"

He held out his hand to Sarita.

"You have told them the news?" he
asked. "That you have not waited in vain?
That your persistence has met its reward?"

"Oh, you devil!" cried Sarita, in a voice
of indignation.

Whereat the other laughed his most genial
laugh. "Possibly, my dear? But what
woman ever objected to that?"

He stared straight into Sarita's eyes.
Hers fell; and then, after a pause, he turned
to the others, still smiling. "You see," he
said, "the life-force has pursued me, it has

dragged me out, it has made me a slave once more! It has compelled me to become a moral man. Against my will, against all my intellectual convictions, I have to fulfil its purposes. For this reason I come to ask for mercy, and forgiveness of the past. I am, as you know, one of the two surviving members of the pre-revolutionary regime— one of the two law-abiding citizens still left in the world! But I am willing to recognize the *status quo*. Sarita tells me that Billy and Helen have a baby. I suppose that may be described as a part of the *status quo*. She tells me also that there has been a divorce."

He looked at Helen, who answered, " There has."

" I forgot to inquire as to the particulars, but I presume that means that you have some authority to which I can apply for admission to your state. Have you a governor, for example? "

" We have not needed a governor," said Billy. " All we needed was a judge, to pronounce the decree of divorce."

" And who was the judge? "

" Sarita was the judge."

" Good Lord! " exclaimed Granville.

" And in bloomers? " He began to laugh; but then, recovering himself, he addressed the heiress of the Knickerbocker-Smythes. " My dear lady . . ."

" Your Honour," Sarita corrected him.

" Ah, yes, Your Honour. Well, I have made my application for admission to the Co-operative Commonwealth, with all the rights, privileges and immunities of a citizen——"

" Oh, Granville, cut it out," broke in Billy. " You are welcome to come here if you behave yourself."

Granville smiled. " It would seem there is a governor, after all," said he.

Such was the ceremony of initiation.

They went on with the celebration of their May-Day festival. But they could not forbear to question Granville about his struggle with Tuttle, and they found that the topic was one that could not be dropped. Tuttle was in their thoughts, and kept creeping into their conversations. They were sorry for the wretched capitalist, left alone with his greed; they felt somehow that the revolution was not complete until the last person on earth had been converted. For a month or two they argued this question back and forth—until at last Billy made the announcement that it was his intention to take a trip to the city and persuade Tuttle to reform.

The announcement brought much protest, for Billy was the most useful member of the community, and everybody objected to his running the risk. It was going into the lair of a wild beast. If anyone were to go, declared Mrs. Lumley-Gotham, it should be some old person.

" But who is there? " demanded Billy.

" I would go myself," declared the Mistress of Society, " if I knew how to run an automobile." Then, turning upon her husband, " You know how," she said.

Which proposition Lumley-Gotham answered by leaping from his chair, and running to the cellar to hide!

Amid the laughter that followed, Billy announced his intention of starting the next day. Reggie and the Lord Bishop declared that they would constitute themselves a bodyguard, and de Puyster also volunteered, in his capacity as representative of the press. So the next morning the four set forth. They sought out the hotel, and made a cautious entry by the rear way, and stole up the stairs and through the corridors.

They were armed for a conflict, but, as it proved, precautions were needless. They found the President of the Amalgamated Food Tablets Companies, Limited, lying in the hallway in front of the entrance to the food machinery room. They saw his form stretched out, and stood some distance off and hailed him, but he did not answer. At last, Billy made a cautious approach and bent over him; one glance at his form—reduced almost to the condition of a skeleton—told the dreadful story. The last capitalist had starved to death. He had been too lazy to work, so he had perished; and with him perished his system—and the Co-operative Commonwealth reigned for ever after!

UPTON SINCLAIR was born in Baltimore in 1878. Because he was a sickly child, he was mostly self-taught, and he did not attend school until he was ten years old. But Sinclair read voraciously, and in 1892, not yet fourteen years old, he began a special five-year program at the College of the City of New York; to earn money he published stories in magazines such as *Argosy* and even sold hundreds of jokes. After graduating in 1897 he went to work for the magazine publishers Street and Smith, churning out men's adventure stories at the rate of about 30,000 words each week. In 1900, however, Sinclair quit this job and moved to the wilds of Quebec to write his first novel, *Springtime and Harvest*, which he self-published after being rejected by several mainstream publishers. He continued to write and publish novels, sometimes with established companies and sometimes on his own. His interest in socialism led him to the subject of the poor working conditions of the industrial workers of the United States. He explored this in *The Jungle*, which first emerged as a serial in 1905 in *Appeal to Reason*, a socialist weekly. When *The Jungle* appeared as a book the following year, Sinclair became the most famous author in the United States. He was even summoned to Washington by then-president Theodore Roosevelt. (Although Sinclair had so many ideas for the country that an exasperated Roosevelt finally exploded to an aide: "Tell Sinclair to go home and let me run the country.")

With the money earned from *The Jungle* Sinclair started a socialist colony called Helicon Hall in New

Jersey. Another Sinclair, Sinclair Lewis, worked there as a janitor, but the experimental colony failed after a suspicious fire. Upton Sinclair wrote more than eighty books in his career, including *The Brass Check* (1919), which led to the formation of the Newspaper Guild; *Oil* (1927), a novel about the Teapot Dome Scandal; *Boston* (1928), which explored the Sacco-Vanzetti case; the eleven-volume *World's End* series (1940-53), featuring the well-connected world-traveler Lanny Budd; and *The Autobiography of Upton Sinclair* (1962). Sinclair died in Bound Brook, New Jersey, on November 25, 1968.